I0452674

"She Was Dead...

"Her hands still clenched the arm rests
and her legs were twisted against the chair
as though she had made a terrific effort to stand
after the bullet had torn into her breast . . ."

Rennick looked at her and felt sick to his stomach.
Just a few hours ago she had been making
love to him, and they had laughed and danced
together. Now, because she knew him,
she was dead . . .

Anyone who came in contact with Rennick
was marked for murder, and you'll see
why when you read this hard-boiled novel
about a vicious frame-up.

And Dream

Of Evil

TEDD THOMEY

WILDSIDE PRESS

TO PATRICIA

Copyright, 1954, by Tedd Thomey.

1

RENNICK STOOD ALONE IN THE DARKNESS ON THE ROOF. HE
was a large man in a black leather jacket, a large man with
an expression of concentrated anger on his hard face. He
raised his right fist and cursed the handcuff that bound it to
the slot machine. In the moonlight the circle of chrome steel
gleamed around his wrist like a band of ice. The metal
forced a deep, wrinkled gutter into the skin and already his
fingers were beginning to feel numb and fat.

He studied the way the slot machine was attached to the
large hardwood table. Then, wrapping his arms around the
machine's steel flanks, he dragged it and the table across the
roof. The table legs stuttered in protest against the uneven
surface. In a moment, he halted near a few potted palm
trees and a yellow beach umbrella around which were
grouped some spindly iron chairs with curlicue backs.

The handcuff bit into his wrist as he stretched out his
free left hand until his fingertips touched one of the chairs.
He pulled it to his side. He lifted the chair high overhead
and clubbed it at the side of the slot machine where the other
handcuff was fastened in the elaborate steel scrollwork.
Again and again Rennick smashed the chair down. With all
the fury that was in him he attacked the steel, swinging the
chair awkwardly with his left hand, rattling the quarters inside the machine and making the table and even the roof
shudder.

The open mouth of the coin chute seemed to grin at him
as the chair became a tangle of broken iron while the steel
of the slot machine showed scarcely a scratch. He threw the
chair away.

He glanced around, saw the skylight nearby and dragged
the table over to it. Dropping to one knee, he looked down
through the blue-tinted glass. In the cocktail lounge below,
the lights were out, but enough moonlight filtered down to
outline the room's details. He wasn't surprised to see that

the men and the blonde were gone. His glance went swiftly over the objects in the room.

Because of the tinted skylight glass, everything was blue. Even the flow of blood from the cop's head was blue. The cop's torn tweed sport jacket was blue. He lay in the doorway between the small cocktail lounge and the men's room, one leg partly concealing the barrel of a revolver. His blue shoes rested against the porcelain base of the toilet and his blue fingers were curled around the neck of the shattered floor lamp that he'd fought with. Near him lay the girl's open purse and some of its contents—comb, compact and torn Kleenex—had been knocked under the baby grand piano.

Rennick looked away. He felt sick. It wasn't because the cop was dead. He'd seen dead men before. It was the way the bullet had torn in beside the man's ear. Almost exactly the way that .45 slug years ago had killed May.

Rennick sat down. He leaned against one of the table legs, his right arm sticking up crookedly to where the handcuff fastened it to the slot machine. There was pain in his wrist under the tight metal but none in his hand. His hand was numb. With his other hand, he took an unopened pack of cigarettes from a pocket of his leather jacket. He broke a cigarette working it out of the pack. He stuck the bigger half in his mouth and probed his pocket until he located a match. Scratching at the head with his thumb until it flared, he touched the flame to the butt.

In the unsteady yellow light, his face was an irregular pattern of lines and angles. The gray eyes were hard and at their corners was the faint webbing of premature wrinkles. His curly black hair was moist with sweat. Before the match went out, he glanced at his heavy chrome wrist watch. Ten to three. A hell of a lot had happened in half an hour.

His arm was beginning to go numb. He stood up, cursing the handcuffs and as his anger mounted he seized the steel links between the cuffs with his left hand and pulled with the fierce hope that he could separate them with muscle alone. He didn't stop until blood smeared his wrist and the metal band. Then, sucking hard on the piece of cigarette, he leaned across the slot machine and stared off over the flat rooftop.

All around him, a dozen stories below, the city lay sleeping, its street lights dots of brilliance diminishing to darkness

6

in the distance. He could hear an occasional car pass on Ocean Boulevard, the tires whispering up to him softly. Out in the harbor were the rigging lights of two cruisers. He thought about the sea-going Marines snug in their sacks below decks. The lucky bastards. They didn't know how lucky they were.

Hearing a faint whining sound off near Third or Fourth Street, Rennick turned his head. The sound came closer and he recognized it. A siren.

He waited. It didn't seem possible that anyone could have told them already.

The siren came down Ocean Boulevard with a roar and Rennick heard brakes squeak and doors slam in front of the hotel. He turned quickly. He looked down through the sky-light at the revolver under the cop's leg. Too late to get it now. Wrapping his arms around the slot machine again, he dragged it and the heavy table back to the yellow beach umbrella. He picked up another iron chair and inserted one of the spindly legs into the steel opening on the machine where the cuff was fastened. But as soon as he exerted pressure, the leg bent and then broke. Repeatedly he swung the chair—long, shattering blows that made the machine clang and the table rock. He hit his numb right hand and swore as the flesh broke open.

He heard another sound. This time it was a faint whirring sound from the wooden hut that housed the elevator mechanism on the opposite side of the roof. It meant the place would be overrun in a minute with men in dark uniforms.

Rennick dumped the heavy table over on its side. He fell to his knees beside it and folded his arms around the slot machine. Across his back, muscles swelled against the leather jacket as he tried to twist the machine loose from the table. Screws squeaked against oak. He strained until he thought the cords in his neck would burst, but the machine did not move. From the wooden hut, the whirring sound continued without interruption. Rennick drove his shoulder against the flat side of the machine. He hit it again, rattling the coins inside, but the machine would not bulge from the table.

The whirring sound stopped. Rennick glanced at the sky-light. A round spot of light skipped across the blue glass. A

7

flashlight. Before long they would find the steps that led from the cocktail lounge to the roof. He knew he had to get a maximum of leverage on the machine. It was either now or to hell with everything. Arching his body, he scissored his long legs around one of the table legs and pulled on the machine with all his strength. A sliver of wood broke off near one of the screw holes. A crack as straight as a ruler edge sped the length of the table top. The coins inside the machine rattled and clicked like a pocketful of marbles as he wrestled the machine and the table from side to side. He felt the screws give, but not far enough or fast enough. He pulled until he was sure the metal band would sever his right hand—and then the two rear screws pulled out with a screech that almost paralyzed his eardrums.

Down in the lounge someone shouted. Rennick ripped the other two screws loose and picked up the machine. It was heavier than he'd expected. He trotted slowly across the roof, looking for the fire escape that had to be there someplace.

It was over in the shadows on the far side of the building. When he reached it, he shifted the machine to his right arm, propping it awkwardly on his hip. The top section of the fire escape was merely a thin iron ladder, curved where it passed over the concrete parapet to fasten onto the roof. He hesitated and then stepped out onto the first rung. He had a sudden sensation of unreality. It didn't seem possible that this could be happening to him. He saw the tiny lights of the beach walk, far far below him, and he felt frozen in space. He didn't want to go down the ladder, but he forced himself to take the first step. Instantly the slot machine slipped off his hip, a tremendous weight that wanted to plunge straight to hell. Somehow he caught it on his thigh and managed to wedge it against the ladder. One of the screws dropped out and clicked against an iron rung. Then there was a long space of silence before he heard the faint chilling thud of it against the paved beach walk.

He got the machine propped again on his hip, hugging it to his side with all the strength of his right arm. He went down slowly and each time he was forced to move his left hand to a new rung there was a moment when his only contact with the ladder was with his feet. Each time he had the

8

feeling of being balanced on a thread that might break at any instant. Once he looked up, expecting to see men following him, but they hadn't arrived yet. When he was near the bottom of the ladder, the machine got away from him again. It crashed against the open grill-work of the landing, wrenching his arm as he fell on top of it. The handcuff knifed into his wrist. He picked the machine up and went swiftly down the steps. It was a relief to be able to hold the machine in both arms again.

This part of the fire escape was the conventional zigzag iron stairway with pipe railings. Arriving at a second landing, he could hardly believe it when he saw that there was a high iron gate between the landing and the next section of stairs. A chromium padlock on the gate gleamed dully in the moonlight. Rennick swore and rattled the lock, hoping it wasn't fastened. But it was.

He was about a story and a half below the roof. He ran back up a few of the steps to the only window he'd passed on the way down. It was closed, but a poke of his fingers against the upper frame told him it was unlocked. It creaked only slightly when he shoved it up. Setting the slot machine on the sill, he eased his big body up beside it. Flowered drapes got in his way and he brushed them aside. He slipped inside the room, picked up the machine and closed the window. He latched it and drew the drapes shut.

When he turned and faced into the room, it was in total blackness. He heard a clock ticking somewhere nearby.

He stood there, waiting and listening. He blinked against the darkness, but he could see nothing. He waited. He felt sure there was no one in this room, but if he were to knock over a lamp or stumble into a chair he might awaken somebody in a room nearby. He waited a whole minute, two minutes. Then he moved his left hand in an exploring motion in front of him, felt nothing and took a tentative step away from the drapes.

"Stay where you are!" a woman's voice warned.

The words stunned him. She was nearby, only a few feet away at the most, and she must have been there all the time. He started toward her but halted when he heard footsteps on the fire escape outside the window.

A man spoke. A cop. "He didn't get through the gate! It's locked."

From the roof a reply was shouted down, too indistinct to be understood by Rennick. But the man outside the window understood and Rennick heard him move on the steps. In a moment, fingers scratched at the window pane.

"It's locked!" the man shouted.

Rennick stood there stiffly, waiting for the woman to cry out.

Outside, there were more sounds of feet moving on the stairs. Then there was the soft ringing sound of shoes going up the ladder. Then silence.

Rennick stayed where he was, trying to see the woman in the darkness. A corner of the slot machine pressed uncomfortably against his ribs, and as he shifted it the handcuff steel scratched the thick glass of the jackpot and the coins inside rattled briefly.

"What do you want?" It was a younger voice than he thought at first, a girl's voice, and she wasn't afraid.

"Nothing," said Rennick. He wondered why she hadn't called to the cop.

Again there was a long silence. Still trying to see her, he rubbed his eyes with the back of his hand. He was able to make out a dim shadow that looked like a divan and another black object that looked like an overstuffed chair, but there was no shadow with the shape of a girl. He continued to wait. It was up to her to make the next move.

After a moment he heard the rustle of cloth. He realized that what he'd thought in the dimness was a divan was actually a bed. One of two single beds. Moving the covers aside, the girl got up and he heard the rustle of a silkier cloth. Then there was the click of a light switch but the room remained dark. She clicked it again.

"Probably a short," said Rennick. "Some lamps got smashed."

There was another silence. Then he saw her dim outline in a doorway. She was starting to pass through. Crossing the room quickly, Rennick caught her shoulder. Under the thin cloth of her robe, her skin was soft and warm from the blankets.

"I don't want you leaving," he said.

10

"Don't be foolish." She tried to turn away, but he tightened the pressure on her shoulder.

"Anybody else in the place?" said Rennick. "And where's the phone? I don't want you getting too near the phone."

"You're hurting me," she said. "Let go of me."

He removed his fingers slowly.

"That's more like it," she said. "After all, I could have said something to that cop on the fire escape."

"You've got me wondering about that," said Rennick.

"Go ahead and wonder . . ." Her shadow passed through the doorway and there was the soft sound of bare feet on polished hardwood. In the other room, after a moment, glass tinkled.

The slot machine had grown heavier. Picking his way carefully through the darkness. Rennick sat on one of the beds and set the machine down beside him. He wondered why the girl wasn't afraid of him. He rubbed his swollen right wrist and his fingertips came away sticky.

He heard the girl's bare feet pad back into the room. Turning, he looked for her.

"Where are you?" she asked. "I've got something for you."

He tensed, suspicious of her tone, and did not reply.

"Well, where are you?" she said. He could read nothing more significant than impatience into her words.

"On the bed," he said.

She laughed, low and musically. "That's nice . . ."

She came over to him. He realized she was holding a glass out to him, a glass from which came the odor of whiskey.

"I don't use the stuff," he said. But he took the glass and kept it because in the darkness he could see no place to set it down.

"What's the matter—you sick or AA?"

He didn't reply. She remained standing in front of the bed and dimly he saw her raise her own glass and drink from it.

"I guess that's your business," she said.

He stood up, his right arm trailing down to the slot machine on the bed. "How many doors to this place?"

"One."

"Locked?"

"What do you take me for?" Her tone was almost bitter.

She stood quite near to him. He looked down at her but the room was too dark for him to make out her features. He wondered if he should trust her. He would have to. There was no other place for him to go. Certainly not now while the roof of the hotel, its elevators, and stairways were busy with cops.

She stepped closer to him and ran her fingers lightly up the sleeve of his leather jacket.

"Tall, aren't you?"

Her fingers found his free left hand. Taking the glass, she set it down somewhere nearby. Then she took his hand again. Suddenly he was sure he knew why she hadn't called to the cop outside the window.

"They're strong," she said, touching his fingers. "Calloused. What kind of work do you do?"

"I'm a cathead man. Oil work. I handle the derrick lines . . ."

"I like a strong man," she said. "I—"

He pulled her to him quickly, bent down and kissed her. Her lips were warm and her mouth tasted pleasantly of whiskey. Drawing her closer in a half embrace, he could feel that she was small and light. He wondered if she was pretty. She pressed herself hard against him and shivered slightly when he slid his hand down her back to the small soft curve of her hip. When he pushed her robe down over one shoulder, she started to pull away but he held her tightly and kissed the soft perfumed flesh. He could tell that she wore no nightgown under the robe. He sat on the bed, drawing her down with him and she lay across his legs. She turned, started to reach up to him and her fingers tripped against the center links of the handcuffs.

He could tell that she'd discovered the slot machine by the abrupt way she sat up.

"My god!" she said. "What's that thing?"

Rennick laughed at her confusion. "Just an old one-armer."

"Two's company," she said, "but my god that thing's a crowd. How did you ever—"

"Later," said Rennick. He pulled her hard against him, searching for her mouth, but she started to giggle softly.

12

"You can't," she said. "Not with that thing, you can't At least not very well . . ."

Rennick laughed with her. "Maybe I can't take my jacket off, but it has nothing to do with . . ." He pulled her robe further off her shoulder and then they both jumped as a buzzer sounded insistently nearby.

"What the hell!" said Rennick.

"Somebody's at the door." She slid quickly off his legs and stood up.

The buzzer sounded again.

"Don't answer!" said Rennick.

"But I have to. If it's Emil he'll break the door down! He knows I'm here."

"And if it's the cops!" Rennick picked up the slot machine and started toward the window.

"Don't be a fool!" She tugged at his leather sleeve. "There's a better way!"

As the buzzer sounded again, she led him across the room and opened a door.

"Damn it, no!" said Rennick. "Not a closet. It's the first place they'll look!"

"Shut up and do as you're told!" she ordered. "This one's different."

Clothes hangers squeaked against a metal rod as she pushed dresses aside. A latch clicked.

"You have to stoop," she said, shoving him forward. In the complete blackness, Rennick had no idea where he was going. He kicked exploringly with his foot until he felt an opening in the closet wall. Cradling the slot machine in both arms, he bent nearly double and squeezed in through what seemed to be a small doorway. The girl closed a door behind him. Then she shut the closet's outer door and he was left by himself in silence and darkness.

Running his free hand along the walls, he discovered that he was in a space about the size of a phone booth. It was less than six feet high, forcing him to stand with his head partly bowed. He held the slot machine against his ribs for a while, massaging his aching wrist and hand, trying to work out the numbness. After a while he sat on the floor, resting the machine on his jack-knifed legs. He wondered where he could get a chisel and hammer or a hacksaw. It didn't seem

13

likely that the girl would have any tools. The crowded little space began to grow uncomfortably warm. He wished he could smoke but he knew he couldn't risk it.

He didn't want to think about the things that had happened in the cocktail lounge but the events were too fresh, too deeply engraved in his conscience, to be ignored. As clearly as if the man were sitting beside him, he saw how the bullet had gone in behind the cop's ear, just like the one that had killed May. The thought made him feel sick to his stomach and he forced his mind into another channel. He wondered about the man he'd been supposed to meet, Georgetti, and why he hadn't shown up. And the blonde at the piano—he wished he'd gotten a closer look at her. It was her purse that had fallen near the cop's body—

Rennick tensed as he heard the knob turn on the outside closet door. He heard the door swing open, followed by the sounds of heavy footsteps and hangers being shoved on the closet rod. The floor planking on which he sat creaked slightly from the movement of the man on the other side of the wall.

"Nothing in here," the man said. "Try the bathroom—" The closet door closed, shutting off the rest of the words.

Long minutes passed during which Rennick heard nothing but the sound of his own breathing. The air in the small space became stale and foul and he was on the verge of moving out into the main closet section when the door opened. The girl told him to come out.

Rennick groped his way through the doorways into the bedroom which was still in darkness.

"Cops?" he asked.

The girl didn't reply. She was a dim shadow standing by one of the twin beds.

He asked her again.

"Yes," she said, her words dull and lifeless. "Three of them."

"You saved my neck," said Rennick. "Thanks."

Stepping over to her, he reached out and took her hand. Her fingers were tense. She turned from him. She tore her hand away and stepped backward.

Rennick moved toward her and she turned again, running

14

into something that toppled over with a crash. The sound did something to her.

"Keep away!" she said shrilly. "Keep away from me, you rotten murderer!"

2

RENNICK STOOD THERE STIFFLY. HE WAITED FOR THE GIRL to say something more but she was silent.

"Nobody talks like that to me," he said. "Whether I killed anybody or whether I didn't, I don't take that kind of talk from anybody . . ."

As he stepped toward her, she backed away. He reached out and caught her arm. She tried to back further away, stumbled into the bed and Rennick pushed her down upon it. Dropping the slot machine onto the pillows, he pulled the girl to him. She didn't scream. She tried to fight him off but she was no match for him. When he bent over her, bringing his face down to hers, she twisted her head from side to side. He caught a handful of her hair, held her head and kissed her. He kissed her long and hard, crushing her lips against her teeth. Then he released her and stood up.

"That's all I want from you," he said. Picking up the slot machine, he stood beside the bed waiting to see what she would do. He expected her to make a run for the phone or the window. But she did nothing. He groped his way across the dark room and sat in a square overstuffed chair.

Neither spoke for a long time. Occasionally he heard the rustling of cloth as she changed her position slightly on the bed.

"How many rooms you got here?" he asked.

She waited before she replied. "This one and the one out there . . ."

"A kitchen or a living room?"

"A kitchen?" She laughed bitterly. "This place is too swanky to have kitchens."

"Any tools around—a hammer, pair of pliers or a file?"

"No. And why should I help somebody like you?"

15

"You had two chances to turn me in," he said. "You didn't. I don't care what your reason was, but you didn't." The slot machine pressed uncomfortably against his legs and he shifted it.

For another long minute, the room was silent. Rennick massaged his aching wrist and wondered where he could find some tools at this hour of the night. Breaking into a gas station might be the answer, provided he could get away from the hotel without being caught. But that damned locked gate.

"Did you kill him?" the girl asked abruptly.

"Kill who?" said Rennick.

"The cop. When they came in here, they said the man they were looking for shot a cop. I hope you didn't murder a cop, that's all, because if you did they'll get you if it takes a hundred years."

"I didn't murder him," said Rennick. "I'm mixed up in it, but I didn't murder him."

"The way you said that, I almost believe you. Almost, but not quite." She got up from the bed and walked past him, leaving behind the faint fragrance of her perfume. In a moment, he heard the tinkling of ice and glasses in the other room and then her shadow returned. He wondered what she looked like. She wasn't very tall and she was slim, he knew that already: but he wondered about her face.

"Try the lights," he said. "Maybe they've got them fixed."

She flipped the wall switch twice but nothing happened. Then she walked over and handed him a glass. "It won't hurt you," she said. "It's a 7-Up."

"Swell," he said, sourly. "When what I need is whiskey and lots of it."

"Make up your mind," she said. "I fixed you a bourbon and you wouldn't even touch it." She held out her own glass. "Here, take mine."

He couldn't see the bourbon. It was merely a dark shadow in a darker glass. But the good clean odor of it made his nostrils tingle.

"I told you I never touch the stuff." He handed the glass back to her.

"You're not very consistent," she said. As she drank, she

16

remained standing near him. "I don't s opose you'd care to explain the slot machine either."

"I might," he replied. "Two unfriendly guys, I think their names are Sutro and Stanley, thought it would be a good idea if the cops had a patsy all tied up and waiting for them when they got here. They didn't have much time and the heaviest thing they could find to hook me up to was the slot machine and table up on the roof garden. So they used the cop's handcuffs and then they scrammed out of there."

"Interesting, if true," she said.

"Suit yourself," said Rennick.

"I find that most men usually lie," she said.

"It depends on the woman."

She laughed briefly. "I deserved that."

From his pocket, Rennick drew out a few coins. He sorted through them until he felt what he thought was a quarter. Placing it in the coin slot, he pulled the handle. Wheels spun and gears meshed. One by one the wheels stopped spinning. The machine gave out half a dozen evenly spaced clicks and then coins tumbled noisily into the pay-off trough. Rennick counted them. Ten.

"Must've been three oranges," he said.

"Are you that lucky at love?" the girl asked.

"Nope. How about you?"

"No comment," she said.

Rennick played a few more quarters back into the machine before he got up and walked over to the window. Drawing the drapes carefully apart, he looked out. Clouds shielded the moon so he couldn't see much. There was no one on the fire escape—at least not in front of the window. It was too dark to tell whether there were men moving around on the beach ten stories below.

"That god damn gate," he said.

When he turned around after drawing the drapes shut, she was standing nearby.

"I wonder what you look like," she said. "Are you nice or are you mean looking?"

"You could light a match and find out."

"It's more romantic this way . . ." She moved up to him, put her arms around him and he discovered that she was no longer wearing her robe. She was naked and her skin was as

17

warm as her breath. His free arm went around her and his hand found her left breast. It was firm and alive. She pulled his head down, her fingernails digging into the skin on his neck.

"Kiss me," she demanded. "Kiss me hard like you did on the bed!"

Her mouth was soft and moist and her teeth felt even and clean. It could have been a long kiss—but she tore her mouth away.

"My god!" she whispered. "Emil!"

She slipped quickly away, whispering as she fled toward the bed. "Get down! Hide someplace!"

Rennick had heard nothing. He took a step away from the drapes and then paused. In the next room, there was the sound of a door being closed slowly, deliberately. The catch snicked shut.

There wasn't time to make it to the closet. Rennick remembered that the overstuffed chair stood in a corner of the room. He got to the chair without knocking anything over and slipped around behind it. He had hoped there would be room enough back there to kneel so the chair would shield him, but there wasn't and he couldn't risk the noise of shoving the chair forward. Shoulder-blades against the wall, he stood there hugging the slot machine to his chest and waited.

A man's footsteps came into the bedroom. A hand groped for the wall switch and Rennick hoped the lights were still out. The switch snapped a few times, the room remaining dark.

"Josey! Wake up!" The man's voice had the bite of authority, as if used to being obeyed.

The covers rustled. "What?" She was pretending she'd been asleep and not doing too good a job of it. "Oh, it's you. What do you want?"

"I got some questions to ask—and you better give the right answers!" There was a sharp slapping sound, the sound of a hard palm smacking a buttock, and the girl gave a little yelp of pain.

The man crossed the room and threw aside the drapes. For a moment, he stood still, looking out, then he returned to the bed.

"Did you see him?" he demanded.

18

"See who?"

"You know who I mean. The guy on the fire escape."

"I've been asleep . . ."

"The hell you have." He slapped her again, harder this time, but she did not cry out.

"Through all those sirens and the running around on the roof—you're lying!" Again the sound of flesh meeting flesh reverberated throughout the room.

Still the girl did not cry out. Rennick clenched his teeth.

"The police woke me up," she said. "And then I went back to sleep—"

"When I find that guy I'll blow his guts out." The man crossed in front of the chair and opened the closet. He went inside and Rennick heard him open the inner closet door. After a moment, he came out.

"Lucky for you!" he said. "God damn it, the hotel's lousy with cops looking for him. There's no telling what they'll find. Maybe they've already found something—and if they have there'll be hell to pay. And if you're lying to me, Josey—"

"I-I'm not lying—" Her voice was muffled by the blankets.

"All right, get some clothes on. I'm holding a stockholders' meeting in five minutes and I want you down there!"

The man left the bedroom. The door opened and shut in the outer room and again there was silence, except for small sobbing sounds on the bed. Rennick went over to her.

"How did you ever marry a slob like that?" he said. "Another two seconds and I'd of thrown the slot machine at him and to hell with the consequences!"

"He would've killed you," she said. "He wouldn't have thought any more of it than shooting a cat."

Rising from the bed, she began to dress. Rennick looked at the luminous dial of his watch. It was nearly four.

"Wasn't he kidding about holding a stockholders' meeting?" he asked.

"No, Emil never kids. If he called a stockholders' meeting on the moon at midnight, every last one of them would be there—on the minute."

"He sounds like a first-class bastard."

"He is."

19

"I'd like to have had him in my platoon at P. I. We'd of rubbed his snotty nose in it a few times."

"P. I.?"

"Yeah, Parris Island, where I was a drill instructor."

"Oh?" She finished dressing and came over to him. "I've got to go now but I've got something for you."

She handed Rennick a key. It felt too light to be a door key.

"What's this for?" he said.

Her laugh was low and amused. "I believe you mentioned something about a gate?"

"Christ!" he said. "You had it all the time! I could've been a hundred miles from here by now. I could've unloaded this pile of iron!" He shook the coins in the slot machine. "I could've dropped it over a cliff by now!"

"I know . . ." she said softly. "I didn't want you to."

"To what?" Rennick started toward the window.

She hesitated. "To leave."

"Is that why you didn't turn me in?"

"I don't know. I guess so."

"What's wrong with your husband?"

"Emil's not my husband."

Rennick pushed the drapes apart and began to ease the window up. "I guess that's your look-out."

The girl remained standing in the shadows near the bed. She took a few steps toward the doorway and stopped. "Are you going to tell me your name?"

He decided not to, then changed his mind. "Rennick."

"First name?"

"John."

"Will you come back?"

"I don't know."

There was a pause.

"I hope you will . . ." she said.

As the window slid up, it creaked slightly and he was unable to hear the rest of what she said. He waited, but she did not speak again and he assumed she had gone. Placing the slot machine on the sill, he put his head out the window and studied the zigzag lines of the fire escape all the way down the side of the building. So far as he could tell, there was no one on it. Craning his neck, he glanced up at the

20

roof. The ladder was clear. He sat on the sill, swung his legs over and stepped out on the landing. At the same moment, clouds low over the dark ocean melted from in front of the moon and he saw that he'd been wrong. He wasn't alone on the fire escape. The shadow of a man sat on the dark iron steps about seven stories below.

Moving slowly to keep the sounds to a minimum, Rennick climbed back through the window. He sat on the sill and lit a cigarette. He knew he should be more worried and he couldn't understand why he wasn't. Maybe it was because it was impossible to believe that it had all happened. The girl— she was hard to believe. But the things that had happened in the cocktail lounge—they were real enough. He'd been a fool to go up there in the first place and a bigger fool for even talking to Sutro and that other guy, the fat one they called Stanley. It had seemed like a good idea at the time but it didn't now. He snubbed the cigarette out against the window pane and watched the feathery ashes float out into space. He was in it now and there were things to be done. He had to cut the god damn slot machine off his wrist and find that blonde, the one who'd been sitting at the piano when the cop got shot. Again he thought of the way the bullet had torn into the ear—just like it happened to May. His mouth twisted bitterly. Christ, it was a hell of a thing to have happen to a man twice in one lifetime.

He looked out the window again at the man on the fire escape. As he watched, the man got up and made his way slowly down the steps to the bottom landing, jumped off and walked down the alley. Rennick watched until the man was just a dim dot moving across the beach.

Slipping out through the window, Rennick lifted the slot machine to his chest and went down the few steps to the iron gate. The chrome padlock and the key were new and shiny and worked easily. After he passed through, he closed the gate and locked it. He went down the steps as swiftly and quietly as possible, occasionally looking up to see if he was being followed and looking down to make sure that no one else was coming up. He noticed that the window at each landing was closed and wondered if the hotel's tenants all were against fresh air or were merely taking precautions against second-story men. When he reached the first floor

21

level, he knelt and set the slot machine on the iron grillwork. He went a few rungs down the short ladder that hung over the alley, and then let go, giving the machine a healthy tug.

Dropping about five feet, he landed on the paving and at the same moment caught the slot machine as it fell. The steel jerked painfully around his wrist and he couldn't hang onto the heavy machine. It hit the pavement with a thump and a rattle of coins.

He picked it up and looked around. The sound hadn't attracted anyone. He decided not to go down on the beach but to head for Ocean Boulevard where he might break into a gas station for tools. Moving in the alley's shadows, he passed a battered group of sickeningly sweet-smelling garbage cans and a caved-in cardboard box which had once contained cartons of cornflakes.

The sound of running footsteps made him twist around. A man was rushing toward him, his unbuttoned trench coat billowing back and slapping against his pumping legs.

Rennick ran as fast as he could but the machine cut his speed in half. Before he'd gone twenty-five yards, he could hear hard breathing behind him as the man drew closer. It was a race Rennick obviously couldn't win. He stopped, turned around and braced himself.

The man came closer. He carried no gun. He wore a snap-brim hat on the back of his head and ran with the lumbering step of a heavy man who wasn't used to much running. He could've been a cop, a businessman, or a well-dressed hoodlum and he surprised Rennick by running past with hardly a sideways glance.

Rennick drew to a halt. He hesitated and then began to walk on down the alley, watching the man ahead until he was an indistinct shadow that mingled with the dark shapes of the boulevard. Before he'd walked much further, Rennick heard new sounds behind him and turned again. Another man was running down the alley behind him and this time there was no question of identity. The man wore a dark uniform and there was a glimmer of metal on his chest.

He drew a gun out of a leather hip holster when he was within a few yards of Rennick.

"All right," he said. "All right!"

It was a warning but Rennick ignored it. He darted to

the cop's side, swinging the slot machine. The cop was young and Rennick saw a flicker of hesitation in his eyes. The cop easily dodged the clumsy blow of the machine and struck at Rennick with the revolver butt. The metal raked Rennick's neck. He grabbed the cop's gun arm with his free left hand and aimed a kick at his groin. The blunt toe of his oxford went into thigh muscle the first time—but the second kick was accurate. Clutching his lower belly, the cop fell on his side, writhing slowly.

"You dirty son of a bitch!" He tried to tilt the revolver up to bear on Rennick, but Rennick jerked it out of his grasp. As Rennick dropped the gun into his jacket pocket, the cop managed to blow a shrill blast on his whistle. Rennick pulled the whistle from the cop's tight lips, ripped the chrome chain from where it was attached to the uniform shirt pocket and flung it into a pile of tattered newspapers.

A glance down the alley told him the damage had been done. Already the shadowy shapes of other cops, at least two, were moving up the alley toward him.

Running back the way he'd come, Rennick passed under the fire escape. It was a temptation but he knew the slot machine would prevent him from leaping up to the ladder. He sprinted along the flank of the hotel, his shoulder brushing shrubbery and squatty palm trees growing in a strip of earth along the alley. He noticed that there were small windows behind some of the shrubs. Branches clawed at him as he went up to one of the windows. He swore when he saw that it was covered with new wooden shutters. The other windows were also covered. He ran a few steps farther until he came to a door. It was padlocked and new boards lay on the cement walk before it; apparently the door window was to be shuttered also.

Using the slot machine as a battering ram, Rennick smashed the glass out of the window. Concealed by the shrubbery, he couldn't see the cops but he heard them coming closer and knew that they had heard him. He climbed in the window, gashing his hand on glass fragments that remained in the frame. In the darkness it was impossible to tell what kind of a room he was in. He smelled oil and wondered if it was a furnace room. He walked quickly, arm outstretched to act as a buffer, and immediately tripped over

23

some concrete steps. As he hurried up them, he heard the cops at the broken window. He went up a dozen steps, groped along a landing, went up a dozen more steps and ran into a door. The knob turned easily and he pulled the door open a crack. Outside was a hall and it looked deserted.

Rennick slipped through the door, closed it gently and moved down a corridor dimly lighted by fixtures streamlined into the walls. He moved soundlessly across a cushiony wine-colored rug, past closed doors marked "Business Office" and "Cashier." A carpeted stairway led off to his right and he climbed it swiftly, turning once to see if he was being followed.

The stairs led to a mezzanine landing. He heard a door open suddenly nearby and immediately he sprinted through open French doors into a large dining room. It was deserted and the tablecloths in the dimness were like whitecaps on a dark sea. He thought he heard someone coming up the steps he'd used a moment before and he moved swiftly across the dining room and through two swinging doors plated with brightly polished copper.

He found himself in a kitchen. Rows of bluish fluorescent lights burned overhead but the room seemed unoccupied. A large dishpan full of yellow corn on the cob stood on the brown linoleum. Near it was a wooden box heaped with loaves of bread and a crate of half-gallon cartons of milk. A gleaming white refrigerator with scores of doors ran along one wall. Along another wall was a battery of chromium and black gas ranges.

Rennick looked at his wrist watch. It was nearly four-thirty. The cooks would probably be coming in before long to start breakfast. He walked across the kitchen and out a side door that led to a small coffee shop. About a dozen blue leather stools ran in a row before a polished blonde birch counter. Some of the stools had been taken off their spindles and rested on their sides on the floor. Cardboard boxes, a few broken dishes, and a box of spilled matches littered the counter top. There was dust on everything.

He shifted the slot machine in his arms uncomfortably and as he did so it occurred to him that what he needed might be in the kitchen. He went back into the kitchen and began

24

pulling open the wooden drawers in the cabinets below the sinks.

He found a drawer full of long, handled carving knives. He found a drawer containing an assortment of cleavers. Then he found a drawer containing ladles, pancake turners —and a bone-saw with a steel blade.

3

RENNICK TOOK THE SAW AND WALKED BACK TO THE DARKEST corner of the coffee shop. Pushing aside a broken, gold-edged cup and saucer, he set the slot machine down on the counter. Where his right wrist was pinched by the handcuff there were smears of dried blood. His hand was completely numb. The fingers were thick and stiff and a white waxy color except for the dark residue of oil under his rough nails.

The metal of the cuffs themselves was a good quarter of an inch thick and he knew it would take a long time to cut either of them. The three-linked chain between the cuffs was considerably thinner. He chose the center link and set the saw to work. The chain was fine tempered steel and the first few strokes scarcely scratched it. Bearing down harder, he was rewarded with a shower of steel dust which floated from the blade down to the floor.

He wished there was some way he could muffle the metallic rasp of the saw's small teeth. Engrossed in what he was doing, he was caught completely off guard by the frothy skirt which suddenly swept near him.

Rennick stopped sawing and looked at her. He wondered how long she'd been in the room.

"Hello," she said.

Rennick didn't reply. He picked up the machine and took a step toward the door. The girl looked at him curiously but she didn't seem very excited or concerned about what he was doing. She was a striking natural blonde wearing a strapless evening gown that revealed creamy white shoulders and considerable cleavage. He couldn't understand why the slot machine and the handcuffs didn't bother her. It occurred to

25

him suddenly that she must already have known about him. She must be the girl he'd met in the bedroom.

"Are you Josey?" Rennick said.

"No . . ." She shook her blonde head and said in almost a sing-song tone: "My name's Laurette and I'm—"

Rennick waited for her to finish the sentence, but for some reason she didn't bother. She stepped closer to him. She was young, not much more than nineteen or twenty. Her hair was a gleaming pale yellow upswept neatly on one side, held in place by gold combs and allowed to fall carelessly over the left side of her forehead. She had the beautifully clear complexion of the true blonde and wore no make-up except a coral lipstick. Her gown was an emerald green with a sweeping ruffled skirt and she wore high-heeled gold slippers. In her right hand she held a glossy red rubber ball to which was attached a long rubber band.

Rennick placed the slot machine back on the counter. Picking up the saw again, he inserted the blade in the tiny cut he'd started. As he moved it back and forth, he continued to watch the girl. She let the red ball fall and it swung from the elastic cord in her hand. He wondered if she was the blonde who'd been at the piano when he'd shot the cop up in the cocktail lounge, the one who'd lost her purse in the scramble after the lights went out.

"Were you upstairs?" said Rennick.

She nodded her head, her blue eyes watching him curiously.

Rennick kept the saw moving back and forth.

"Did you see what happened?" he said. "I mean the gun and everything?"

"I was upstairs playing."

There was something strange about the way she said it, something Rennick couldn't pin down.

"Did you lose your purse?"

She shook her head. "I just kept playing."

'You must have lost your purse," said Rennick. "I saw it later. It was lying right beside the guy."

Holding the elastic cord in one hand, the girl bounced the red ball on the floor with her other hand.

Rennick removed the saw from the chain link. Blowing

26

the steel dust away, he saw that he'd cut not more than one-sixteenth of the way through.

"What are you doing that for?" she asked. "Why are you tied up?"

Rennick looked at her sharply. He wished he hadn't been so busy with Sutro and Stanley. If he'd just taken a closer look at the girl at the piano.

The blonde bounced the ball up and down.

"What'd you do after you left the piano?" Rennick said.

"Piano?" she said. She dropped the ball and picked it up.

"For god's sake quit fooling with that thing and pay attention!" Rennick dropped the saw and grabbed her arm. "Were you playing the piano up in the lounge or weren't you?"

Her clear blue eyes widened. "I don't think so. I don't think I know how to play the piano . . ."

Rennick scowled at her. "You just said you were up there playing it. Make up your mind!"

"Did I say I was playing it?" she said.

He wasn't sure whether she was being sarcastic or not. There was something about the way she said things that had him stopped. He put his face close to hers and sniffed, but there was no odor of liquor. Her eyes were large and blue, rather vacant looking, but the pupils seemed normal enough.

Releasing her arm, Rennick stepped back to the counter and picked up the saw. The girl watched the blade move back and forth and then she threw the red ball up in the air and caught it. She threw it again and missed. When she bent over to pick it up, he couldn't help noticing how exquisitely formed her breasts were.

She held the ball out toward him. "Would you like to play with it?"

Rennick shook his head. He watched her carefully as she moved along the counter rearranging the broken dishes in an irregular line and tracing lines in the dust. He couldn't understand it. At first when she'd come in, he'd figured because of the evening gown that she'd just left a party here in the hotel. The red ball could have been some kind of a party favor. But now he wasn't so sure. She was too preoccupied with the ball. It seemed to mean a great deal to her.

"What did you say your name was?" he asked.

27

"Laurette." She wound the elastic cord around her slim wrist.

"Last name?"

Delicate frown lines appeared between her blonde eyebrows. "Grazo," she said, after a moment.

It was hardly the kind of a last name he expected. She certainly looked Swedish or Norwegian.

"Where do you live?"

Laurette shrugged. "Here. I live right here."

Blowing more dust from the cut in the chain link, Rennick saw that he was about a quarter of the way through.

"Would you like to play with me?" Laurette asked suddenly. She walked up behind Rennick and put her arms around him.

Rennick kept sawing at the link.

"Wouldn't you like to play with me?" Laurette asked again. Keeping her arms around him, she stepped around and looked up into his face. There was nothing coquettish or flirting in her wide blue eyes. They seemed childishly innocent.

"What do you mean play with you?" said Rennick.

"Oh, just play," she said, quite simply.

"For god's sake," said Rennick. He tried to push her away, but she clasped her fingers together.

"The other boys play with me all the time," Laurette went on.

"What do they do?" said Rennick.

"Oh, they dance with me sometimes. And sometimes they take my clothes off." She spoke without a trace of embarrassment.

Rennick swallowed dryly. He laid the saw down on the counter. Very carefully, he parted her fingers and pushed her arms from around his waist.

"I don't like the way they play sometimes," she said.

"Yeah," said Rennick, "I can imagine." He stepped away from her. He had a pretty good idea now what was wrong with her.

"How much is nine times five?" he asked.

She tilted her head impishly on her lovely neck. "Nine times how much?"

"Nine times five. Simple arithmetic."

28

Her eyes grew hurt. She said nothing.

"What's a Democrat?" said Rennick.

Laurette kept looking at him, her eyes vacant.

"Is the earth round or square?" said Rennick. "Who was Adolf Hitler?"

Her lower lip began to tremble. "I don't know . . . I just don't know—but please don't be mean to me, please don't."

"It's okay," said Rennick, "it's not your fault." He picked up the saw and inserted the blade in the cut. "I've got work to do. Maybe you'd better run along and play with your ball."

"Aren't you going to play with me?" Tears sparkled at the corners of her eyes.

"I've got work to do," said Rennick. "Go on now. Beat it."

"Please?" She tried to put her arms around his neck.

"For god's sake!" Rennick tucked the saw under his arm and picked up the slot machine. He left the coffee shop and returned to the kitchen. Laurette followed.

"Beat it!" said Rennick angrily. "I'm not kidding. You're in my way."

Laurette turned away from him. Her shoulders quivered and she began to cry quietly. Green skirt swirling about her legs, she ran across the kitchen and out the copper-plated swinging doors into the dining room. Rennick watched the doors swing back and forth, gradually decreasing their activity until they stopped swinging altogether.

"The bastards," he said softly, "the dirty bastards."

He noticed that she'd dropped her red ball on the floor. He picked it up and put it in his jacket pocket on top of the revolver he'd taken from the cop in the alley. It occurred to him that she might return or she might tell someone she'd seen him here. On the far side of the kitchen there was a solid-looking wooden door. He went over to it, tripped the iron handle and walked into the chill of a large cold storage room. He made sure there was a handle inside before he let the heavy door bang shut. His breath hung lazily in the air like steam on a cold winter night and he hoped his leather jacket would keep him from freezing until the job was done. He walked past sides of fatty beef hanging from hooks on

29

the wall over to a thick, blood-stained chopping block where he set down the slot machine.

There was a heavy-bladed hacksaw hanging on the wall near the chopping block. It looked twice as efficient as the small bone saw he'd been using. As soon as he started moving it back and forth in the cut in the link he could tell he was making progress. He bore down with all the strength of his left hand, hoping the storage room's thick walls would muffle the blade's rasping bite.

It took him about ten minutes to cut the rest of the way through the first side of the link. Maintaining a steady rhythm with the saw, he went to work on the second side. When he was three-quarters of the way through, he saw the handle on the big wooden door move. It might be Laurette; or it might be someone else.

He picked up the slot machine, transferred it to his right arm and got the revolver out of his jacket pocket. He got over to the door just as a dark-haired busboy stepped in. Rennick hit him once on the top of his head. The busboy turned, gave him a blank look and toppled to the floor. A small, ragged piece of paper fluttered from his fingers and landed in a pile of sawdust nearby. The heavy door swung shut pinching the busboy's legs which were half inside the storage room and half out.

Grabbing a handful of the busboy's starched white jacket, Rennick dragged him inside and let the door slam. The busboy's glazed eyes were half open and his tongue was out, resting unsanitarily in the blood-stained sawdust. He was a high-cheek-boned Mexican with a mop of coal-black oily hair, pale olive skin and sideburns that nearly met at his Adam's apple.

Rennick returned to the chopping block. It took him five more minutes to cut the rest of the way through the link— and then he was free. From the machine at least.

He held up his cramped right arm and moved it around, rubbing his hand to try to get the circulation going. The steel cuff, with a small bit of cut chain attached, remained around his wrist, but it didn't feel nearly so tight now. When he turned, he was nearly knocked over by the lunge of the busboy who had suddenly come to life. They crashed against the chopping block, knocking over the slot machine. It

30

thumped to the floor behind the chopping block, bringing a side of beef down on top of itself as Rennick gave the busboy a shove that sent him flying backward across the room.

The busboy spit out some sawdust, swore in Mexican and came back waving his fists. Rennick slugged him on the side of the head with the revolver, a little harder this time than before. The busboy did a half-spiral, as graceful as any tight-trousered ballet artiste, and sprawled in the sawdust.

Rennick picked up the scrap of paper and read what was written on it: "Wating in 419. L." The words were printed in a childish uphill slant which explained the misspelling. The "L" undoubtedly stood for Laurette. He put the paper in his pocket and opened the heavy door a crack. The kitchen was still deserted. He left the storage room but when he was halfway across the kitchen he turned around and went back inside. Hooking his fingers in the busboy's jacket, he dragged him outside. There was no percentage in letting the boy freeze to death, even if leaving him in the kitchen meant he'd be discovered sooner.

Passing through the dining room, Rennick headed back toward the stairway. He wondered where he would find the blonde who'd been at the piano. He swore. The Charlemagne was a big hotel. She could be in any one of a thousand rooms, or maybe she was all the way to Northern California by now.

Farther on down the hall, a door opened and Rennick froze in his tracks. A man came out of one room, crossed the corridor and went into another room. Rennick thought the man looked familiar.

After waiting a moment, Rennick went on down the hall. One of the doors was open a few inches and he stood near it, listening. He recognized the voices.

"By god, I tell you it's the only thing to do," Sutro was saying.

"And I tell you it ain't," said Stanley.

"Okay, if you're so damn smart, then how many times has Emil been wrong?"

"Emil's gonna screw things one of these days," declared Stanley confidently. "Nobody can do all the things he's been doing and get away with it all the time."

Rennick moved closer to the door, so he could hear better.

31

"I tell you the boat's the deal," said Sutro. "There's nothing like lots of water between you and the law."

One of the men opened a door inside the room and there was a pause before they spoke again. Rennick glanced around the hall to make sure he was still alone.

"I don't swim so good," complained Stanley. "Once I fell out of a boat when I was a kid and I nearly crapped my pants I was so scared."

"If I know you you didn't just nearly," said Sutro.

There was another pause before Stanley spoke again. "Okay, so maybe I did. I was just a kid."

Suddenly Sutro's voice was in the hall directly behind Rennick. "Stay right where you are, buddy."

A powerful hand grabbed Rennick's right arm and hammer-locked it up behind his back while another hand poked something small and sharp into his kidney. Rennick swore and tried to turn around but the hammer-lock was too good.

"Go on, try something!" said Sutro. "I'll blast your backbone into jelly!"

He shoved Rennick through the door and into an untidy but well-furnished room where Stanley was lying on a divan, his shoes off, a bottle of beer clutched in one fist.

"Christ!" Stanley jumped to his feet. "I didn't even know you was gone!"

Rennick looked at the door to the adjoining room which was open, explaining how Sutro had sneaked up on him. The bastard had gone through the other room and out a door farther on down the hall.

"See what he's packing!" ordered Sutro, and Stanley dutifully went through Rennick's pockets, removing the revolver he'd taken from the cop, his worn black leather wallet, the shiny red rubber ball, and his car keys.

Stanley grinned a fat lopsided grin and bounced the ball on the floor. "Funny thing for a cop-killer to be lugging around!"

He wasn't as tall as Rennick but he was nearly six feet. There was a lot of belly on him and his blue-striped shirt was bunched up and wrinkled around his middle. A few inches of the zipper on his fly were open. He turned suddenly and threw the ball at Rennick's head. It grazed Ren-

32

nick's neck and knocked over a table lamp, cracking the pottery figure of a nude girl which formed the stand.

"I'll handle him," said Sutro. He released the hammer-lock, stepped around and faced Rennick. He had good shoulders, a thick neck with many lines criss-crossing in leathery skin, and a face that looked like it had been stepped on, run over, kicked and chewed down through the years. He was as tall as Stanley but where Stanley was suet Sutro was muscle. In his right hand there was a heavy army-style .45 and without warning he slapped it against the side of Rennick's jaw.

Rennick was only able to duck the blow partially. It felt like half his face had been torn off. He touched his jaw with his fingers and they came away red.

"God damn but what the cops wouldn't give to have you!" said Sutro. He laughed low and without humor, deep in his throat.

Again he swung the pistol. He was a fast, nervous man and though Rennick ducked, the barrel cracked the bone in his elbow, sending waves of electricity painfully up his arm.

"I don't work the way the average guy works," Sutro explained. "Some guys ask the questions, get no answers and then they go to work. Me, I mess the guy up first—and then I ask the questions. Saves a lot of time."

He looked Rennick over, considering where the next blow might do the most damage.

"You hit me again," said Rennick, "and I'll stick that .45 right up your behind!"

"Just you try it, buddy," said Sutro. "Just you try it." But he stepped back a few inches, his eyes slitted and glittering.

They studied one another for a moment. "Where's the slot?" Sutro demanded.

"So soon?" said Rennick. "I thought you messed a guy up first!"

"You're asking for it!" warned Sutro.

"Yeah!" said Stanley. "We'll tear your guts out, gut by gut! Now tell us where that slot is!"

"Why don't you wipe the beer off your face," Rennick told Stanley pleasantly.

The fat man growled and started to move in, but Sutro grabbed his shirt sleeve. "Not yet."

33

"Balls!" said Stanley, but he stayed where he was.

Keeping the .45 trained on Rennick's stomach, Sutro stepped over to the end-table where they'd tossed the objects rifled from Rennick's pockets. He tossed the billfold to Stanley and told him to look it over. Then he picked up the .38.

"Police Special," he commented. "You've been a busy little son of a bitch, haven't you?" He broke the revolver open and spun the chamber. "Loaded, so I know damn well this isn't the one you killed the cop with. Besides I made damn sure that one was under his leg."

Stanley opened the wallet's compartments over the end-table, dumping out currency and papers. "Thirty bucks in bills," he announced, "a card in the Oil Workers' Union, driver's license, a couple of stamps and what the hell is this?"

He held up a newspaper clipping. "Brother, get a load of this. Got his picture on it and everything."

"What's it say?" asked Sutro.

"It says the President gave this bum a medal for being a hot shot at Iwo Jima. It says he got the Cong—, the Congressional Medal of Honor for shooting up a bunch of Japs." Stanley turned to Sutro. "What in the hell's a frog-man?"

Sutro didn't reply. He was busy scowling at Rennick. "Well, ain't you the two-bit hero? Carrying the clipping around all the time. I'll bet you're a wow at every bar. I'll bet you'll read that damn thing to any drunk that'll listen. I know your type. You get a couple of beers in your gut and you're the bawling hero that has to talk over every pimple you ever got shot off your butt!"

Rennick went after him. He didn't think Sutro would be dumb enough to trigger off any shots with the hotel still busy with cops. He got the first punch in, a cruncher that drove Sutro's Adam's apple against the back of his neck. Sutro went back a few steps, shook his head and came charging in while Stanley circled around to the rear.

"Son of a bitch!" yelled Sutro. He swung the heavy .45 like a club at Rennick's skull and missed. But Sutro was fast and as the pistol butt sang past the side of Rennick's face, Sutro's left fist came tearing in from far away, spinning

34

Rennick's head around till he could feel his neck bones crack. At the same moment, Stanley's arms came from behind, and clamped around Rennick's chest in a giant bear hug. Before Stanley could hook his fingers together, Rennick pivoted halfway around, got one arm in a nutcracker around Stanley's head and tossed him over his hip. But he'd taken too much time with Stanley and he got a terrific wallop across the head from Sutro. His knees turned to gelatin and he sagged and got another whack on the head with the pistol butt. He reached out and seized Sutro's right ear. He pulled with all the strength of his strong derrick man's fingers and heard Sutro howl. Cartilage snapped and tore under his fingers and the ear stretched like rubber. Sutro's howl turned into a high-pitched scream and blood squirted like soda pop all over the side of his face. Rennick lunged for the .45, the force of his lunge carrying both him and Sutro into an end-table which collapsed into matchwood. They landed on the floor together, Sutro's ear still firmly pinched between Rennick's fingers. He looked around for Stanley and found him just as the polished pointed toe of Stanley's brown oxford belted him in the jaw. The blow rolled Rennick over and he had to let go of Sutro's ear. He got to his knees and then stood up and started trading punches with Stanley. He buried two or three blows up to his wrist in the soft layers of Stanley's belly and then felt new pain across the back of his head as Sutro went to work with the pistol butt again.

It went on for a long, long time. He kept swinging and dodging and poking and weaving at them and though they struck back hard and often he no longer felt their blows. He danced around lightly, leading with his left and countering with his right, surprised at how easy it all was. But then abruptly something was wrong. Bright daylight was streaming in through the room's windows; and it was impossible because he knew it wasn't even dawn yet. He discovered that he was lying on the floor. He swung his fists again and saw that it was quite useless because Sutro and Stanley were no longer in the room. The door to the hall was partly open and the room was a shambles but Sutro and Stanley were gone, definitely gone. Rennick felt sick to his stomach. He turned, cradled his head on a crushed lamp shade and went to sleep.

35

He dreamed of water and danger. The water was a midnight blue as dense as ink and he was swimming in it with arms as heavy as lead. Something grabbed his ankle and pulled him completely under. A mackerel went swimming by, its scales gleaming like jewels and its wet slimy tail fins brushed his face. An empty fifth of whiskey floated by with something obscene written on its lavender label. When the army-style .45 automatic came by, Rennick screamed but it was a soundless scream because his mouth was full of water that tasted like blood. The .45 swam in circles around him, its blue steel butt undulating like the fins of a fish, the single dark eye of its muzzle staring at him coldly. Two dismembered heads came floating by, their hair swirling in the dark water. One was the cop's head. The other's was May's. As each head came past, it turned so Rennick could see the bullet hole black and red near the ear. Rennick screamed and screamed, tasting the blood that ran into his mouth and into his eyes and into his ears, especially his ears . . .

4

WHEN RENNICK WOKE, HIS HEAD ACHED WITH THE FIRES OF hell and his mouth was caked with dried spit. He sat up, rested awhile and then got slowly to his feet. Every joint was stiff and he felt like an old man. A glance at his watch told him it was seven a.m. and that meant he'd been knocked out and sleeping it off for at least two hours. An early-morning breeze came in through the open window and sent the curtains shimmering out over the radiator. He noticed that the door to the hall was still partly open. Sutro and Stanley must have left in a hell of a hurry and it was a wonder people passing through the hall hadn't looked in, noticed the wreckage, and called the management.

He hunted through the smashed bits of pottery lamp and end-table until he located his car keys and wallet. He knew the revolver he'd taken from the cop in the alley would be missing and it was. Under an overturned chair he found the newspaper clipping. Without reading it, he folded it and placed it in his wallet. He noticed that Sutro and Stanley hadn't taken his thirty bucks. Which could mean they'd merely forgotten—or were so loaded themselves that thirty was just small change. Before he left he picked up the red rubber ball and dropped it into his jacket pocket.

He wasn't sure what his next course of action should be. Maybe he might be lucky enough to find a vacant room where he could hole up for a few hours. What he needed was a shave and a shower and a change of clothes. The black leather jacket and tan gabardine slacks were a dead giveaway.

The corridor was as deserted as it had been a few hours before. When he passed the French doors that opened onto the dining room, he noticed that although the chandeliers were burning, all the tables were unoccupied. Maybe it was still a little too early for breakfast in a hotel as ritzy as the Charlemagne. A man in a white jacket came out through the copper doors that led to the kitchen. He walked hurriedly and Rennick could hear him talking to himself.

"My god!" the man said.

Rushing out the doors and down the stairway to the first floor, the man was too upset to notice Rennick. As Rennick glanced back into the dining room, another man in a white jacket came in through a side entrance and went immediately to the kitchen doors. Carrying a small jar, he disappeared into the kitchen.

Rennick crossed the dining room and peered into the kitchen through one of the small windows in the copper doors. Four or five cooks in tall white floppy hats and busboys in white jackets and black trousers were gathered around a man on the floor. Their faces were horror-stricken.

"My god!" said the man with the jar of smelling salts. "He's dead!"

One of the men stepped away momentarily and Rennick got a good look at the man who was lying there. It was the Mexican busboy with the long sideburns. His face was a sickly, olive-green color.

"The man and the box is what she said!" one of the men was explaining. "I was right there when she said it. She said he hit Rudolpho on the head with a gun!"

Rennick looked again at the busboy. This time he looked

for the small signs of death and they were there, though there was no blood on the white jacket—or anywhere, for that matter. But the jaw was slack and the eyes had rolled upward, exposing half moons of white under the unmoving eyelids.

Fists clenched at his sides, Rennick turned quickly. He crossed the dining room and went back to the corridor. He felt sick. He told himself that he couldn't have hit the boy that hard, he couldn't have. But he knew that the second blow had been a good one because he'd meant it to be. Without realizing exactly where he was going, he went up the carpeted stairway, passing landing after landing, floor after floor. A record kept spinning around in his head, playing the same hollow words over and over. *"You're running up a good score, Rennick. You've killed three good American citizens now. Would you like to try for four? You're running up a good score, Rennick. You've killed three good—"*

He met no one on the stairs. After a while he walked down one of the corridors branching off to the left. It was the seventh floor, judging by the numbers on the doors. The corridor was as deserted as the stairway and dining room had been. It occurred to him that it was a hell of a hotel if so few people stayed here. Maybe they were all late risers. He went indiscriminately from door to door, giving each knob a gentle turn. After he'd tried a dozen or more knobs, he found a door that was unlocked. Before going in, he looked carefully up and down the hall. As he glanced at the window at the end of the corridor, a man in a familiar dark blue uniform passed by on the fire escape. It was nice to know the bastards hadn't forgotten him.

The room was large, with two windows, and obviously unoccupied if the bed, which had neither blankets nor pillows, was any indication. No clothes hung in the closet. There was no soap or towel in the bathroom. A search through the drawers of the tall limned oak dresser proved it to be empty, except for a bottle of good bourbon in the back of a lower drawer. There was about an inch of liquid in the bottle.

Rennick sloshed the liquor around. He held it up to the light, admiring its color, and ran his tongue lightly over his lips. It was exactly what he needed. He pulled the cork and

38

tilted the bottle up to his mouth. But he remembered the clipping in his wallet and lowered the bottle slowly. Dropping the bottle back in the drawer, he slammed it shut with a vicious kick. He went over, lay on the bed for a moment and got up again. There was too much nervous energy running through him to let him relax.

He went into the bathroom and took a shower. Even though there wasn't any soap, the water cut some of the dried sweat off his body and the heat and steam were good for the aches in his muscles. He dried himself with his green sport shirt, patting the skin gently where it was bruised and purple around the steel bracelet on his right wrist. After he was dressed, he opened the medicine cabinet and found a black plastic razor someone had discarded. The blade was rusty and didn't look sharp enough to cut water. He stepped back into the shower and picked up a sliver of Palmolive that he'd noticed stuck in the drain. It didn't work up much of a lather but the blade was sharper than he'd expected.

The face that looked back at him from the mirror over the washbowl was tired and beat. The circles under his cold gray eyes looked like they'd been stamped in black ink. There was a cut where his curly dark hair was parted and another gash on his jaw where Sutro had slugged him with the .45. There were cuts inside his mouth where the skin had been knocked against his teeth.

He felt a little better after he was cleaned up. From his pocket he drew out the scrap of paper the busboy had lost. "Waiting in 419. L." He wondered if Laurette could have put on an act for him with that rubber ball and "play with me" business. If she were the blonde who'd been playing the piano when he shot the cop, maybe she had some reason for covering up. If he could just find that blonde, part of his troubles would be over. He looked again at his watch. It was seven-thirty. He laughed bitterly. He was supposed to report to the rig in half an hour. The driller would be running around like crazy when he didn't show up. Well, to hell with him. He didn't like the driller and the driller didn't like him and anyway he could get a job, cathead or lead tong, with any derrick crew on the hill.

Making sure the door was closed but unlocked, Rennick left the room and went down the corridor to the

39

staircase. When he got to the fourth floor, he found room 419 with no difficulty. He tested the door knob and it turned easily. He stepped inside, eased the door shut and looked around. Once more he found himself alone.

The room was a drawing room, beautifully furnished and part of a suite. The walls were painted gold and some of the chairs and the love seat were polished blonde wood upholstered in green and white striped brocade. Several comic books were scattered across the polished surface of a library table. Near them was a blonde doll. She was about 20 inches tall and stood by herself. She wore a black negligee so transparent that her black panties and black bra could be seen underneath.

Rennick crossed the room, noticing that parts of a Tinker Toy set were lying on one of the chairs next to a man's blue and white checked sport coat. Passing through French doors, he went into the bedroom and then he stopped and sucked in his breath.

They were lying together on a big robin's egg blue Hollywood bed. Wearing an undershirt and nothing else, Stanley was sprawled at an angle across the girl. His fat greedy face was lying on his bent arms. There were two bullet holes in his back, heart high. Laurette lay on her back, her lovely slim legs tangled in Stanley's. The fine spun gold of her hair fanned brightly across the pillow and she wore nothing but a small gold heart locket around her white throat. Very little blood had flowed from the hole in her temple. The sight of her perfect coral-tipped breasts, rising so proudly, caused something to tear inside Rennick. He wanted to seize Stanley's fat obscene body and rip it into a million shreds. He wanted to set fire to the shreds so there'd be nothing left to remind him or anyone else of the things that had happened here.

Rennick looked away. His stomach turned over biliously and he knew that the only thing that kept him from vomiting was the fact that he'd had nothing to eat for hours. He went over to the bedroom window and looked down at the white foaming surf.

"The sons of bitches," he said. "The dirty, rotten, sons of bitches . . ."

He realized that the bitter odor of burned powder still
40

permeated the room and that meant they hadn't been dead very long. He stepped over to the bed and touched the slightly bent fingers of Laurette's small hand. They were still warm. He knew he had to get out of there. Whoever had done this job might have left the door unlocked deliberately and was waiting nearby for some sucker to wander in. Maybe the cops had already been tipped off and were on their way up. Rennick left the bedroom. *If they tie me to this one,* he thought, *I might as well stop running right now.* As he went out the door to the corridor, he carefully wiped the inside and outside brass knobs with his handkerchief. He was certain that he hadn't touched anything else. Nothing except Laurette's small hand.

He went down to the third floor and along the corridor to the window that opened on the fire escape. Sliding the window open, he looked out. There were no blue uniforms in the alley but he swore when he caught sight of one at the top floor level. He debated whether he could get down to the alley before the man on top could give the alarm and decided he couldn't. Closing the window, he returned to the stairway. Somehow he had to get out of the hotel, even if it meant walking out the main entrance in broad daylight. He went down the steps to the first floor hall and out into the lobby, passing under the great gold and green chandeliers which hung from the lofty ceiling, making a circuitous path around the brass-studded, brown leather chairs and divans which were parked on the green frieze rug. As he approached the two heavy panes of glass which formed the ultramodern front doors, he hesitated, then veered away from them to the left. A black and white patrol car was parked in the loading zone in front of the entrance and two cops were in the front seat. Rennick strode past a florist shop, past a small gift shop, hoping he looked like a man who knew where he was going. A side door led to a coffee shop. He opened it and went inside.

In contrast to the deserted, dusty coffee shop on the mezzanine floor, this one was a hub of activity. In booths along the wall, scores of businessmen discussed the day's big deals over toast and coffee. Shop girls waved cigarettes and dabbed at their bright mouths. Rennick made his way past busy waitresses to the only vacant stool at the long counter

41

and lit up a cigarette. Among all these expensive worsteds, tweeds and over-plaids, he felt conspicuous in his leather jacket. He wished he were wearing a hat. He kept his head down and his eyes glued on the menu until the waitress took his order for coffee and hot-cakes. He could tell by the curiosity in her eyes that she was wondering about the cuts on his face. When the plates were set down before him, he ate slowly, observing much of the activity of the room in the large, blue-tinted mirrors behind the counter.

The three men in the booth back of Rennick's stool got up and left. A moment later, it was occupied by a man and a striking blonde. They began a rather heated conversation and despite the general hub-bub in the room, fragments of what they were talking about carried to Rennick.

". . . not all right!" the girl declared, her voice rising. "I don't mind about the stock deal so much, but that deal with the boat is no good!"

Rennick grew tense as he recognized her voice.

He shot her a glance in the mirror. It didn't seem possible that she could be Josey, the girl in the top-floor room. But he knew that voice. They'd talked for nearly an hour in the darkness and though he hadn't been able to see her, he knew all the husky little overtones of her voice. But it was impossible that Josey could be that beautiful, that poised and sophisticated-looking. She'd made it very plain what she'd wanted from him last night. He'd pictured her as some kind of a young hotel tramp, the tinsel and too much mascara type. But, god, this woman was different.

Rennick sipped slowly from his coffee cup. Over its rim he looked again at Josey in the mirror. Maybe her hair was tinted, but if it was somebody had done a hell of a good job. The strands were a gleaming, clean yellow drawn back smoothly from her high forehead and moving in straight long lines to the nape of her neck where they became large loose curls held by a brilliant gold barrette. She had large, intelligent gray eyes in which there was much concern now as she argued with the man across the table. Her mouth was soft and expressive, curving redly over perfect white teeth. She wore a blouse of a rich yellow color, a clinging jersey material that outlined her breasts in bold lines. They were fine up-tilted breasts, not too large and definitely not too small. It

42

occurred to Rennick suddenly that he knew how firm they felt, that he'd run his hands over all the slim lines of her body without knowing in the darkness what wonderful lines they were.

He had difficulty swallowing his coffee. He didn't understand how he could have been such a perfect fool. She'd offered it to him—and he hadn't taken it. She was unquestionably the loveliest woman he'd ever seen and he'd been given a chance to bat .1000 with her—and he'd struck out on the first pitch.

He watched her tilt a glass of tomato juice up to her lips. She set the glass down. It was an ordinary enough gesture, a woman putting an ordinary cylindrical tumbler down on a polished hardwood table top. But there was something in the way she did it, something in the way her wrist curved that drove deep inside Rennick. *God damn it,* he told himself, *I've got to have another chance. I don't care what it costs me, but I've got to have another chance with her.*

Toying with his food, he sat there while the seats on both sides of him became vacant and then reoccupied. He listened to snatches of Josey's conversation.

"I don't think it's too risky," the man who was with her was saying. "She's built for speed, and she'll outrun anything in the water."

It suddenly occurred to Rennick that the man's voice was familiar too. He'd been paying so much attention to Josey he hadn't realized that her companion was Emil, the boy friend who'd slapped her around last night. Looking Emil over carefully, he decided he hated his guts. There seemed to be good shoulders under the expensive draping of Emil's gray flannel coat, although there was also a hint of plumpness and flabbiness at his throat. The wings of his white shirt collar were small and neat and he wore a dashing red and gray striped tie. He had straight dark hair parted in the center over a broad, sloping forehead. There was a touch of gray at his temples and judging by the back of his neck he got his hair cut every week. He had a plump, juicy-looking mouth and clear polish shone on his fingernails as he patted his lips with a paper napkin.

"—all settled then," Emil declared, placing a coin beside

43

his plate. He got up, motioning for Josey to follow, and strode toward the cash register.

She stood, turned slowly and looked into the mirror. Her cool gray eyes met Rennick's in the glass for just an instant. She winked. It was a slow, deliberate wink and there could be no question about its being intended for him. It was completely out of character for the tall sophisticated creature she seemed to be—yet it was completely in character for the person who had clung to him last night. Picking up her purse, she moved slowly, gracefully after Emil. Rennick lowered his eyes to a piece of cocoanut cream pie under a transparent cover and he kept them there until he knew that Josey and Emil had left. It was obvious that she'd recognized him and he wondered how she'd managed it since the room last night had been as dark for her as it had been for him. He wondered if she could have been the blonde at the piano. If she was the one, she could save his neck. Damn it, he had to talk to her—and the sooner the better.

He finished his coffee and lit another cigarette, debating whether to go back into the lobby or whether to make another attempt to leave the hotel. A group of men rose from a long table at the rear of the coffee shop and his decision seemed clear-cut. There were more than a dozen men in the group, businessmen who'd just completed some kind of a breakfast meeting. In a ragged squad formation, they headed for the front doors. Rennick dropped a dollar bill beside his plate and got up, timing things so he stepped unobtrusively into the center of the group and moved along with it. The two men just ahead of him were arguing about the horsepower of refrigerator motors, while the trio behind chuckled over some small joke. He kept in step as they passed through the doors and out to the sidewalk. From the edge of his eye he noticed that one cop was still sitting in the patrol car at the curb. He wondered where the other one had gone. He was glad that the businessmen didn't choose to walk directly past the car. Moving in groups of twos and threes, they turned left and headed downtown. He stayed with them for more than a block, keeping his eyes straight ahead, waiting for the shout or the sound of a motor starting up that would mean trouble. After five minutes, he began to breathe more easily. The businessmen gradually dispersed, but by then it didn't matter. The sidewalks were busier here with shop girls and tradespeople hurrying to work and Rennick concealed himself in the throngs. He walked down Ocean Boulevard to Lincoln Park where crowds of elderly people were already beginning to gather around the roque courts. Choosing a bench on which three old men were seated, he sat down and folded his arms across his chest.

He needed time to think.

5

AT TEN A.M., RENNICK WAS STILL SEATED ON THE BENCH and the little old man with the words "God First" penciled on his ragged hat was still talking about paints and varnishes. Rennick watched one of the elderly men on the sandy court stoop, sight in carefully and swing his heavy mallet with a short expert stroke. The crack of metal on wood echoed across the small park and the large hardwood ball shot against the concrete side of the court, caromed off at a forty-five-degree angle, struck another concrete abutment, spun wildly and came to rest in front of a metal wicket. There was a small pattering of applause from the old folks on the benches around the court.

"Spray, spray, spray," declared the little man with the blue veins in his nose. "That's all these modern painters know. Psssss-ss-t here! Pssss-ss-t there! And they think they've got a job!"

"Yeah," said Rennick.

"Damn right," said the old man indignantly. "Back in the days when I got my card, it took a man six months just to learn how to hold the brush. These young punks these days call themselves journeymen. They wouldn't know a good pig-bristle paint brush if it come up and spit in their eye!"

"I guess so," said Rennick. He was thinking about Laurette and the busboy. Stanley's death and the cop's—maybe

45

there was justice in those. But Laurette and the busboy were different. Just as May's had been different.

A dark green panel truck pulled up to the curb nearby and a young man got out. He strode briskly over to a metal rack on the sidewalk and placed a couple of dozen newspapers on it. The headlines were big and black. Several old men and a white-haired woman ambled over and bought copies. After a while, Rennick went over and dropped a dime into the rusty tobacco can. He returned to his seat on the bench. He wasn't surprised at the things that were in the paper. Nor did he blame the police for being excited over the killing of one of their officers; after all there was no way for them to know what had really happened. There was a statement from the Chief of Police in which he reported that all available manpower was searching the city from the waterfront to the back country and the hunt wouldn't halt until the officer's killer was brought in. There wasn't much of a description of the wanted man. He'd been seen running in an alley near the Hotel Charlemagne; he was a big man in a dark jacket, who might be handcuffed to a slot machine. A more complete description of him would be given to the public as soon as it could be compiled.

Rennick made sure that his jacket sleeve concealed the band on his wrist. He noticed that the old man sitting beside him had changed topics.

"Just like it says in Genesis," said the old man. " 'My spirit shall not always strive with man, for that he also is flesh.' And there are plenty of other ways of saying it that are just as good, right?" He nudged Rennick in the ribs with his elbow.

"Yeah," nodded Rennick, opening the paper up in order to follow the article on an inside page.

"And I'll tell you something else," said the old man. "I've never had a day of trouble in my life and I'll tell you why. Just a few simple rules is all. 'If thou art wise, thou wilt take care of thine own house. Thou wilt cherish thy wife, thou—' "

The old man paused, then spoke sharply. "You look like the kind of fellow that ought to listen to this." Rennick kept reading the paper but that didn't stop the old man. " 'Thou wilt cherish thy wife, thou wilt nourish her, thou wilt clothe

46

her, and thou wilt nurse her if she is ill. Fill her heart with joy during her whole life and be not severe—' "

"I'm not married," said Rennick.

"Well I was—and I lost my wife," said the old man. He paused, then went on. " 'If thou seekest responsibilities, apply thyself to being perfect. If thou takest part in a council, remember that silence is better than an excess of words—' "

"Now there," said Rennick, "there you've got a point."

"Glad you finally agree with me," said the old man. He continued his recitation, but Rennick wasn't listening. Far down in the story, the .38 revolver was mentioned. The police were tracing its serial number and a check was being made of the fingerprints on it. It would only be a question of time till they located the bar where he'd taken it. He wondered how complete a description of him the bartender would be able to give the police. Reading the rest of the way through the article, he noticed the police mentioned that a woman's purse, black leather with a gold buckle, had been found beside the officer's body. In it was a wallet, keys, a fountain pen, some glasses and some postcards.

"Howl ye," the old man declared, grasping Rennick's arm and looking at him fiercely, "Howl ye, for the day of the Lord is at hand; it shall come as a destruction from the Almighty. Behold, the day of the Lord cometh, cruel both with wrath and fierce anger, to lay the land desolate; and he shall destroy the sinners thereof out of it!" The old man shook Rennick's arm. "Are you ready, sinner? Are you ready to die?"

Rennick folded his paper. He withdrew his arm gently from the old man's grip and stood up. "I don't know," he said, looking down into the old man's serious blue eyes. "I was the dumbest kid in my Sunday School class but one thing always stuck in my head. 'The wicked shall perish.' I always kind of thought they meant me."

He walked down the concrete path, leaving the old man nodding his head. Several pigeons waddled boldly along in front of him, picking up bread crumbs someone had thrown down for them. He opened the paper again and reread the part about the blonde's purse. A wallet, keys, fountain pen, glasses and postcards. The wallet or the postcards might

47

have her address—maybe even a picture of her. If he could just get one look into that purse.

Rennick went into a drug store across from the park and dialed the police station from a phone booth.

"Sergeant's desk," announced a tough male voice.

"My wife lost her purse last night at the Charlemagne," said Rennick. "I was reading in the paper about a purse that was found and I thought that might be hers."

"Hold on," said the sergeant. "I'll transfer you."

The line clicked a few times. Then a new voice said: "Detective Bureau."

Rennick swallowed dryly. He hadn't counted on being switched to the brass right off the bat, but he repeated the business about his wife losing her purse at the Charlemagne.

"Yeah," said the detective, "we've got a report on it. Just a minute."

Rennick waited ten or fifteen seconds. He was quite sure the delay meant they were tracing the call. He was on the point of hanging up when the detective spoke again. "Yeah, there's a report on it. How come your wife hasn't been down to pick it up?"

"She has to work today. We need the money that's in the wallet and—"

"Your name Georgetti?" asked the detective.

Georgetti again, thought Rennick. The name of the man he was supposed to meet last night.

"Uh, Sullivan," said Rennick. The detective spoke again but Rennick didn't understand him because a voice interrupted in the background in the detective's office. He figured it was the police radio because there was a lot of static and the voice was brittle and metallic.

"No, a leather jacket. Black and fairly new . . ."

The radio voice cut out as abruptly as it had cut in.

"You still there?" said the detective.

"Yeah."

"Well, like I said, you'll have to come down to the station and identify the purse. We can't give you information over the phone. Tell me what it looked like, and I might save you the trouble."

"No," said Rennick. "I'll come over and look at it." He hung up.

He didn't have the slightest intention of going to the station. It was obvious by the detective's tone that the purse was a trap—and the phone line had been tapped. He was sure of that. Leaving the phone booth, he went out a side door of the drug store, removing his leather jacket as he went. He slung it over his arm, looking for possible places to discard it as he walked down the sidewalk. He wished he weren't wearing the Kelly green sport shirt. It made him feel as conspicuous as an Irishman on St. Patrick's Day. At the next corner there was a super drug store with a row of phone booths near the lunch counter at the rear. Stepping into a booth, he removed his cigarettes and matches from the jacket's pockets. He opened the phone book and traced through the Gs till he came to Georgetti. Two were listed —a Joseph Georgetti on Rivo Alto Canal and a Frank Georgetti on Daisy Street. The Daisy address sounded too trashy. The kind of money there was in this deal sounded more like Rivo Alto Canal. Before he left the phone booth, he tore the page out of the book and stuffed it into the pocket of his slacks. He wrapped the leather jacket in the newspaper and returned to Pine Street. At the first trash can, he disposed of the package. Farther on down the block he went into a men's wear store and bought a tan woolen slipover sweater for $5.98. That left him with about $23 in his wallet. There was no telling how long it would have to last.

When he left the store, a Naples bus was loading passengers at the corner. He swung aboard and took a seat in the crowded center section. Twenty minutes later he got out on Second Street and walked into the residential section. It was just the kind of a suburb a man like Georgetti would choose to live in. All the streets had Italian names. The general pattern was circular because of the canal which curved gracefully through the community's center. Speedboats, cruisers and sailing smacks were tied up in front of the large, swanky homes. Cadillacs were parked in the back yards.

Rennick walked across the concrete bridge which arched over the canal. A few blocks further on he came to an address which matched that on the page he'd ripped from the phone book. Georgetti's house was a pale orchid color, two stories of ultramodern stucco magnificence. The venetian blinds on all the large picture windows were drawn. Palms and monkey tail trees, fig vines and a dozen varieties of shrubs were landscaped around the house. A cream and gold cruiser was tied to the small floating pier in the canal a few yards from the front steps. Rennick went in through a side gate and up onto the broad, blue concrete porch. He punched the button beside the door several times. Chimes rang faintly inside, but no one came to the door.

He stayed on the porch for a few minutes, studying the houses nearby. There seemed to be little activity around them. In a way, he was glad that no one answered the door. What he wanted was a chance to look the place over and try to figure Georgetti's tie with the deal at the hotel last night. There must have been something in the blonde's purse that linked her to Georgetti—a letter, a card in the wallet or something—otherwise the cop wouldn't have mentioned that name over the phone. Leaving the porch he crossed the front yard and went through another gate into the rear yard. A concrete block wall surrounded the yard and there was a two-car garage at the far end. The garage doors swung idly in the morning breeze, revealing that there were no cars inside. He went up to the house's back door and experimented with the shiny brass knob. The door was locked and it was too solid to be tampered with. A few empty crates were lying near a clothesline pole. He stacked them under a window and climbed up. The screen was aluminum with a tough aluminum frame, securely latched.

Rennick jumped down from the boxes and walked back across the neatly trimmed lawn to the garage. He went inside. Hanging on a wall beside a pair of discarded tire tubes was a small rusty handsaw. He took it down off its nail and walked back across the yard to the stack of boxes. Climbing up to the window again, he used the tip of the saw like a knife on the aluminum screen, ripping the mesh with short, deft strokes. Once he heard a sound in the alley outside the brick wall. He stopped his work with the saw and waited. Nothing happened. As far as he could tell, no one in any of the neighboring homes was showing the slightest interest in what he was doing. He finished ripping the screen and folded the cut section back like a curtain, exposing the whole lower half of the window and part of the top half. Tapping the glass with the hardwood handle of the saw, he increased

50

the pressure until the pane cracked. A few more blows and he broke a fist-sized hole in the window beside the latch. He unlatched the window, raised it and climbed in. After he was inside he shut the window and drew the blind.

He found himself in a large yellow bedroom furnished with a shag rug as white and fluffy as new-fallen snow. There were white spreads on the broad twin beds and opposite them stood Mr. and Mrs. chests that were a luminescent green with glass tops. One wall was entirely occupied by a gigantic garish oil painting that was out of character with the rest of the room. It was a life-sized picture of a bulgy muscled man lifting a huge bar-bell. He wore a G-string, oil on his skin which highlighted his muscles and nothing else. His expression was one of extreme confidence. There was something familiar about his face—but Rennick couldn't quite place it. He left the bedroom and went out into a hall. He stopped walking and listened.

Muffled music came from somewhere in the house—it sounded like a radio playing.

It meant the house was occupied—unless Georgetti had gone away and left a radio on. If there was someone in the house, there was no sense kidding around. He'd come to see Georgetti and the sooner he talked to Georgetti the better. And the sooner he got a line on the blonde, the sooner he could do business with the police.

"Hey!" shouted Rennick. "Anybody home?"

There was no answer. The music kept playing.

He went into the living room, his glance traveling rapidly over the pale green love seat and the two rose-colored contour chairs. The music sounded nearer but he could see no radio and the console television set was turned off. He went into the dining room but the music sounded farther away in there so he returned to the living room. Someone was singing now and the sound was easier to trace. He crossed over to the coat closet near the front door. The singing was definitely coming from behind the closet door and it no longer sounded like a radio. It was a woman's voice. She was singing the Toreador's song from *Carmen* in a soprano voice.

Rennick tried the closet door. It was locked. He turned the key that was in the keyhole and then opened the door. A brunette was sitting inside on some wooden cases. Her dark, liquid brown eyes looked up at him in mild surprise but she kept right on singing. The Toreador's song was never intended for a soprano and she was a lousy soprano at that. She kept waving a half-empty fifth of whiskey in time to the music.

She stopped singing, "Hello?" she said. Then she started singing again.

Rennick put his hands in his pockets and watched her. The half-empty bottle explained everything. The brunette was more than just slightly tipsy. She wasn't the perfect beauty that Josey was—but she was still a hell of a good-looking girl. She was deeply tanned with a small pert nose, long Italian eyelashes and a mouth that was soft with bold, full curves. Most of her red lipstick was around the lip of the bottle. Her hair was dark, almost black, cut so short it fluffed out in loose, careless curls around the smooth oval of her face.

"You like it in there?" inquired Rennick.

The girl nodded and stood up, weaving slightly. He noticed that she'd been sitting on a partly opened case of whiskey. Another case of whiskey was beneath the top one. He also noticed that the dress she was wearing, which was as black as sin, fitted her slim curved figure in a way that made sin look very good.

"Who locked you in there?" demanded Rennick.

The girl looked at him and shrugged her shoulder, the shoulder that was partly exposed because her dress had slipped down.

"Georgetti?" said Rennick.

The girl mocked him. "Georgetti?" she asked.

"Yeah," said Rennick. "Did Georgetti lock you in there?"

"I'm sure I don't know what you're talking about." She stuck her pert nose in the air, put one hand on her hip and swept past him in a huff. The pose was quite theatrical and she carried it off well until she walked into the wall, dropped her bottle and sloshed whiskey all over the floor.

" 'Scuse me," she said to the wall. She picked up the bottle and zigzagged her way over to one of the rose-colored contour chairs. She sank down into it, half-sitting, half-lying, her black skirt revealing a good deal of leg. She had fine legs,

52

not as well turned as Josey's, but good enough to get by at Atlantic City.

Rennick walked over to her. "I don't think you're as drunk as you're trying to make out. I think you can tell me who Georgetti is and what his tie-in with the Charlemagne is."

She looked up at him, suddenly coquettish. She handed the bottle up to him. "Have a little drink?"

Rennick looked at the clear amber stuff and his throat muscles contracted. He handed the bottle back to her. "You need it more than I do," he lied.

She shook her head. "That's not what I need."

"Let's quit horsing around," said Rennick. "Who in the hell are you and what are you doing in Georgetti's house?"

"Well, aren't you the tough guy!" She stuck her tongue out at him. "My name's Chili and what're you going to do about it?"

"Chili what?"

"Chili's enough for you," she said. "Plenty for you."

"What are you doing here in Georgetti's house?"

She laughed. "This isn't Georgetti's house."

"It's in the phone book."

"You believe everything you read?" She seemed to notice for the first time that her skirt was pulled up. She smoothed it down around her legs.

"Let's knock off the double-talk," said Rennick. "When's Georgetti coming back?"

"Not for hours," Chili said. "Maybe not for days."

"And you'd be locked in the closet all that time? A hell of a lot of sense that makes."

"What's wrong with that?" She fluffed up her loose dark curls.

"Don't you want to get the hell out of here?"

"Why should I? I live here."

"Then why were you locked up?"

She lowered her eyes demurely. "Because I was a naughty girl . . ."

"To hell with you," Rennick rubbed his hand across his eyes. He felt tired and frustrated. He seemed to have been on this treadmill for days, running, running, and going nowhere.

53

"You sure do a hell of a lot of swearing," Chili said. She set the bottle on the rug beside her chair. "But, you know, you're kind of good-looking in a tough way. Curly hair and tall. Too bad you've got such a chip on your shoulder."

She picked the bottle up again and tipped it to her lips. When she put it down, her brown eyes had a faraway glaze.

"Do you believe in . . . love?" she asked. She closed her eyes and crossed her long legs. Her dress edged up a few inches.

"Maybe," said Rennick. He noticed that she had small trim knees and the skin was very tanned under the sheer nylons. There was a dark 50-cent-sized bruise on her thigh. It occurred to him that the women he'd met since this whole thing started last night had a lot in common. There were the two blondes, Josey and Laurette. Josey had been very emphatic about what she wanted, almost from the start. Laurette had been just a child, a child with a beautiful, mature body. And now there was a third one—a brunette this time—and again the same frankness, this time with a leg show and a bare shoulder. He decided to see how much of her was talk and how much was action.

Taking the bottle away from her he set it on the rug and took her hand. The coral-tipped fingers were limp and unresisting. He shook her arm.

"Hey," he said.

Eyes still closed, she lay there quietly, her breasts rising and falling gently. She'd either fallen asleep—or passed out.

"Hell," said Rennick. He turned away from her and walked back across the living room, through the hall and into the bedroom. He started pulling out the drawers on the Mr. and Mrs. chests. Once he looked up at the oil painting of the man with the exaggerated muscles and the bar-bell. The expression on the face meant something—but he couldn't be sure just what. Pulling out drawers and slamming them shut, he went through both chests until he finally found what he'd hoped would be there. It was an automatic, a heavy .45 in a yellow leather holster. Sliding it free, he turned it over and pulled the clip. There were only three copper-nosed slugs in it. He snapped the clip back into position and checked to see if the safety was on. It was. Whoever owned the gun took good care of it. There wasn't a spot of rust on it and the oil film was fresh and light. He put the holster back in the drawer and—carrying the pistol—returned to the living room.

He sat down in the other contour chair near Chili. Still asleep, she hadn't moved. Her right arm slanted down limply to the floor. He put the chair back as far as it would go and locked it in position with the metal lever at the side. It felt good to stretch out. He laid the .45 on his chest and folded his arms comfortably across it. Absent-mindedly he gazed at the painting of the yellow Chinese junks over the flagstone fireplace. He wondered why he was always in trouble. Killing the cop wasn't so bad—that was something that had to be done. But the little busboy—that was rotten. The busboy hadn't lifted a finger against him. He'd probably never hurt anybody. He was just a young Mexican boy with probably a fat Mom and Pop and a sweet little dark-eyed sister who would never find out that the man who'd killed him hadn't meant to. And there was Laurette. If he hadn't messed around with Stanley and Sutro, maybe he could've prevented her death. God, he would've given anything to have been there waiting when Stanley came into Laurette's room. The fat slobbery bastard going after a kid like that. He should've ripped Stanley to ribbons. But he hadn't been there waiting and he hadn't prevented anything and Laurette had taken a bullet right where the fair blonde hair curled at her temple. It had always been that way, ever since he was a kid. Everything he'd touched had turned to crap. Even in the Marines. He thought he'd found his place finally, a tough outfit, where he might amount to something. But that business with May had spoiled it all and despite the medal he'd been a hell of a rotten Marine. Well, to hell with them. To hell with them all. Except Josey. With her it was different. If Josey was heading for hell, then he wanted to go to hell with her. He wondered if he'd get to see her again. He thought about the way her breasts had pushed up against that yellow blouse and the cool gray expression of her eyes. He had to see her again and find out more about her. Find out everything about her.

He didn't realize he'd fallen asleep until he heard the scream.

It was twilight dark in the room and he became aware

55

that he'd slept through the whole afternoon. The first thing he saw was Chili sitting bolt upright in her chair, holding her hand in terror over her open mouth. Then he saw Sutro standing in the gloom a few yards away. There was a neat black automatic in his right fist and a look of pure killer's lust on his tough scarred face. His right ear was swollen and as red as a rubber eraser.

"Hello," he said to Rennick. "Hello, you lucky son of a bitch!"

6

SUTRO TURNED TO THE BRUNETTE. "GET OUT OF HERE, Chili. You're in the way."

Dark eyes wide and frightened, Chili left her chair and fled obediently into the bedroom.

"Now then," said Sutro, "before I kill you I'm going to ask you one more time. Where's that slot machine?"

"Go fry your head," said Rennick. He realized that he'd slept with his arms folded over the .45 on his chest. The front sight and part of the barrel were in plain view, but because of the room's dimness Sutro apparently hadn't noticed.

"You figure you're pretty cute," said Sutro. "You'll look a lot cuter with your guts shot out. I want to know where that slot is and I want to know right now!"

Rennick didn't reply. He got his fingers around the butt of the .45 and started shooting. At that range, he could've killed Sutro with the first shot but the .45's trigger had the same feel of another .45's trigger years before, the one that killed May. Instinctively he let the gun drift slightly and the first slug tore a tidy hole through Sutro's already tortured right ear. He pulled the trigger twice more and sent slugs singing past Sutro's head. He wasn't surprised when Sutro, backing up in shock and amazement, fell over the other contour chair. The stunning muzzle blast of a .45 could knock a man over all by itself. Firing wildly, Sutro fell sideways across the chair, his gun arm tangled in one of the chair arms. His slugs punched harmlessly into the floor. Before

Sutro could correct his aim, Rennick sprang on top of him and tore the automatic from his fingers. Cursing, one hand cupped over his ear, Sutro slipped down beside the chair and sat on the floor. Blood leaked out between his fingers and ran unevenly across his wrist and down the lined, leathery skin of his neck.

"I'm going to ask you a few questions," said Rennick. "But first—"

He clipped Sutro on the top of the head with the butt of the .45, leaving a satisfactory gash in the scalp. Sutro howled with pain and shielded his head with his arms. Rennick kicked him hard and accurately in the belly and Sutro's breath came out with a whoosh. He rolled over and tried to kick Rennick's legs but Rennick sidestepped easily. Taking careful aim, he kicked Sutro in the rump a few times, rolling him across the rug like a barrel.

"All right," he said, "where's the blonde?"

Sutro couldn't answer. His face was purplish and he was gasping for breath.

Rennick waited a few moments. "The blonde. Where do I find her?"

Sutro shook his head and started to sit up. Rennick hit him on the head again with the butt of the .45 and Sutro stayed down.

"Start talking," said Rennick, "or I'll cave your head in!"

"Which blonde?" gasped Sutro, moaning and clapping a hand across his scalp.

"The one at the piano when the cop got killed. Was it Josey?"

Sutro shook his head.

"Laurette?"

Sutro shook his head again.

"Who the hell was she?"

"I never seen her before!"

Rennick stepped on Sutro's hand, increasing the pressure until he forced the fingers well down against the rug and could feel the bones give a little. Sutro shrieked as if the hand were breaking but Rennick knew he wasn't inflicting that much pain.

"You're lying!" said Rennick.

57

"No! No! I tell you I never seen her before. She was just a babe that was hanging around!"

"What about Georgetti?" said Rennick. "Does he know who she was?"

Sutro mopped at his dripping ear with a dirty handkerchief. "Maybe. How should I know?"

"You better know," said Rennick. He raised the .45 threateningly.

"All right, all right!" Sutro covered his head with his arms again. "Georgetti probably knows who she is!"

"Where's Georgetti?"

"I guess he's on the boat . . ."

"What boat and where is it?"

"The *Cloud*," said Sutro. "Out in the bay."

Rennick started across the room, halted and looked back at Sutro. "What's with the slot?"

Sutro looked at him blankly.

"Spill it," said Rennick. "Why're you looking for the slot machine?"

"There's a joint in town I'm gonna set it up in," said Sutro.

"You're lying," said Rennick. "And if I find out you lied about the boat, I'll come back here and rip you to hell!"

He crossed toward the hall that led to the kitchen.

"You son of a bitch!" said Sutro, tenderly fingering his bloody ear. "I'll get you for this. I'm not the kind of a guy that forgets. I'll get you, you son of a bitch!"

"Any time you think you're big enough," said Rennick. He went into the kitchen, opened the back door and strode down the steps into the back yard. When he got out in the alley, he paused near an apartment house and examined Sutro's automatic in the light that shone from a kitchen window. It was a .32 with half a clip of ammunition. He stuffed the empty .45 well down toward the bottom of a trash can and then continued on down the alley, the .32 in his pocket rubbing comfortably against his thigh as he strode along. He was reasonably certain Sutro had told the truth about the boat—but whether Georgetti would be on it was another matter. There was a chance Sutro might tip off the cops and they'd be waiting for him when he got out to the boat—but that was the chance he'd have to take. Still, if

58

Sutro and the others were using the boat for some kind of a shady deal they wouldn't want cops snooping through it. So maybe Sutro wouldn't tip the law off after all.

Keeping to the alleys, Rennick walked several blocks across Naples until he came to the sidewalk and iron railing on the quay that fronted the bay. Small waves lapped softly at the floating piers and small boats tied in clusters all along the quay. The sky was dark and moonless. The shadows of a lot of large anchored boats could be seen farther out on the bay. But which was the *Cloud?* He walked along the sidewalk until he came to two boys, probably twelve or thirteen years old, who were whittling sailboats out of redwood shingles. They were sitting under a street light where an avenue dead-ended at the quay.

"You boys know which one of those boats out there is the *Cloud?*" Rennick gestured toward the bay.

The boys looked up at him curiously. "You mean the *Golden Cloud?*" said the kid in the yellow and blue striped T-shirt.

"Yeah," said Rennick.

"Well," said the kid. He laid aside his shingle and walked over to the iron railing. He pointed to a group of boats about five hundred yards off shore. "You see that three-master out there?"

"Yeah," said Rennick.

"Well that ain't it. It's the two-master right next to it about a hundred yards. See it?"

"Yeah," said Rennick. "Thanks."

Walking along the sidewalk, he studied the small boats that were tied up at private piers and floats in front of homes fronting on the bay. There were motor cruisers, sailing smacks and a few rowboats. A rowboat was what he needed. After he'd walked a hundred yards he saw one with oars propped across the center seat. He swung himself up on the iron railing, let go and dropped four or five feet to the wooden float. The force of his hundred and ninety pounds caused the part where he landed to dip briefly under water and he got his feet wet. He untied the boat, climbed in and inserted the oars in their locks.

"Hey!" piped a shrill voice. "That's Mr. Norwood's boat!"

Rennick glanced up at the sidewalk. The kid in the blue

59

and yellow striped T-shirt was pointing at him. Under his breath, Rennick swore. He hadn't even realized he'd been followed.

"Yeah," said Rennick, "I know. I'm borrowing it from him." It wasn't exactly a lie. He would return the boat once his business aboard the *Golden Cloud* was finished.

The kid said nothing more as Rennick pushed away from the float and moved out into the bay with strong, steady strokes of the oars. It was a windless night and there were no large waves to interfere with his progress. He hoped he hadn't made a mistake in borrowing the boat. If the kid decided to tell the owner, there might be hell to pay. It wouldn't help matters any if cops came out on the bay hunting for a missing rowboat. It might have been safer to swim out to the *Golden Cloud*, except that he wouldn't have been able to keep the .32 dry—and there was no telling what he might run into aboard the yacht.

After twenty minutes of rowing, he was close enough to study the ship's lines. She was a long baby, sleek and clean, and she must have set somebody back at least a hundred grand. Her two masts went straight and slim up into the darkness. Her canvas was furled and she was anchored fore and aft. Apparently she wasn't going anywhere for a while.

The oarlocks squeaked each time he bore down on the oars and he knew the sound could carry a long way across the quiet water. When he was a hundred yards from the *Golden Cloud*, he drew the oars from the water and sat in the stern of the rowboat. Using one oar, he paddled the rowboat like a canoe, cutting silently through the water. The silence reminded him of the night landing he'd made on the shore of the Potomac once while training in the Corps. He eased the boat up to the wooden ladder that hung down the yacht's starboard side near the bow. He tied the rowboat to it and then sat there a moment listening. The only sounds he could hear were those of the water lapping at the yacht's flanks and the gentle creaking of the heavy and light timbers overhead. There were no crew sounds—no sounds of shoes on the deck, no voices, no sounds of doors opening or closing. Which didn't mean anything, of course. She was a big ship and the crew's quarters might be far back toward the stern.

Rennick went up the ladder. He stood on the deck, squinting in an effort to see as far as possible through the gloom. A dim light burned fore and aft but the rest of the ship was in darkness. He stood there a full five minutes but he heard nothing and saw no one. Keeping his right hand on the .32 in the pocket of his slacks, he began to walk slowly forward. He passed a canvas-covered lifeboat hung from davits, and ducked under several low-hanging lines. He walked around the bow and then came back along the port side. When he approached the wheelhouse, he stopped and waited again for a few minutes. But still there was no activity. Passing around the wheelhouse and the deserted wheel, he returned to his starting point. He decided to explore the ship's interior. Returning to the wheelhouse, he opened a gleaming, varnished door and went down a short flight of steps to a narrow passageway that ran halfway the length of the ship. Doors to several staterooms were spaced at intervals along the passageway. He moved up to the first one, put his ear near the panel and listened. He heard nothing. No sounds came from behind the second door either, or the third one.

The fourth door was different. A round pane of glass, much like a porthole, was built into it and when Rennick looked through he saw a girl. It wasn't a stateroom as he'd expected. It was a wardroom with several dark, polished mahogany tables with mahogany benches beside them. Brass ship's lanterns hung from the walls, throwing a bright light on the girl who was standing on one of the tables.

It was a long table and she walked down to the far end, knelt and switched on a portable phonograph in a blue leather case. Low music with a strong rhythmical drum beat filled the room. The girl walked back to the center of the table and began to dance. Her feet didn't move much but the rest of her did.

Rennick glanced around the wardroom, wondering who else was there, since the girl danced as if she were playing to an audience of a thousand. The door prevented him from seeing all of the wardroom. His eyes went back to her. Her hair was straight and yellow, coiffured in back in a horsetail effect. *Another blonde,* he thought. *But could she be THE blonde?* She wore a sleeveless black blouse, with a plunging

61

neckline, and tight black satiny shorts cut in a sharp V that exposed a great deal of her hips. Black net stockings accentuated her long muscular legs. Her pumps were ultra high-heeled, made of leather as yellow as her hair. She rolled her hips in time to the sensual beat of the drums and clasped her hands at the back of her neck. Moving her feet in brief side steps, she progressed the length of the table, the smooth rolling motion of her hips speeding up as the music's tempo increased. Turning, she danced the length of the table again, this time keeping her back to Rennick. When she reached the far end of the table once more, she spun around on one leg and it was then that she saw Rennick through the glass.

She left the table in a long-legged leap, ran across the floor and opened the door.

"Well, hello!" She had wild green eyes and her eyebrows were dark exaggerated lines that ran at sharp, cat-like angles up her smooth forehead. She took Rennick's hand and led him into the deserted wardroom. Her fingers were so hot they almost scorched his skin.

She frowned at the .32 in his other hand. "What in the hell's that for? Put it away!"

Rennick slipped the automatic back into his pocket. "Were you at the Charlemagne last night?" he asked.

"Why?"

"You look like the girl I saw there last night."

"I was so drunk last night I don't know where I was," the blonde said. The phonograph was still pouring out its deep drum rhythms. She danced away from Rennick over to the table and come back with two cigarettes and a silver lighter. Poking one cigarette into Rennick's mouth, she lit it with a graceful flourish of the lighter and then lit her own. She danced over to a small built-in refrigerator and came back with two bottles of Coke.

"Nothing stronger than this tonight for Vodka," she declared.

She noticed the puzzled look in Rennick's eyes. "Vodka," she explained. "That's my name. What's yours?"

Rennick refused to tell her but his refusal didn't seem to bother her. She drank her Coke, her eyes watching him over the rim of the bottle. He decided her eyes and the green glass were exactly the same color.

"I'm looking for a man by the name of Georgetti," said Rennick. "He's supposed to be on this boat."

"Let's not talk shop," she said.

"I'm looking for a blonde, too," said Rennick. "A blonde that can help me out of a hell of a lot of trouble."

"I'm a blonde," said Vodka, "but let's not talk shop. Let's talk about something else. Or do something else."

"Like what?" said Rennick.

"Well . . . " she said. Her green eyes suddenly looked greener and wilder. "Do you believe girls need it as much as men?"

Rennick let his eyes travel slowly down the lines of her firm body. "Need what?" he asked, although he could guess what she meant. There was something about the way her red lips were parted and moist-looking from the Coke bottle.

"That three-letter word," she said.

"Yeah," said Rennick, "I think so . . . " It occurred to him that she was still another in the crazy pattern of women he'd met since the trouble first started last night.

"Some men don't need it at all, I've found," she declared.

"If you mean me—" said Rennick. He stepped toward her.

"No!" she said. She raised the green bottle defensively. "Not yet. If you so much as touch me I'll brain you!"

"Oh, you're one of those," said Rennick. "You just talk about it. You talk a good fight but you won't come out of your corner when the bell rings."

"Ring the bell some time and try me," she said. She looked directly into his eyes for a moment, then whirled and went over to the phonograph which was scratching at the end of the record. Adjusting the arm, she started the record over again. As the low drum and quiet trumpets began their rhythm again, she sprang upon a bench and then back to the table top. Her hips began to weave wickedly back and forth. Her lips were parted and her green eyes never left Rennick's face. She danced the length of the table, her graceful movements increasing in tempo as the beat of the drums and trumpets increased. Her long fingers touched the top silver button on her black blouse and loosened it. She loosened two more buttons and the blouse fell open. It was obvious from

63

the way her breasts moved against the thin satiny cloth that she wore no bra underneath.

She turned and twisted with the music and Rennick felt blood pounding in his throat. The girl's fingers moved to the side of the black shorts, touched a zipper and opened it slowly, deliberately. She pulled the shorts down and stepped out of them without losing step with the drums and trumpets. The panties she wore were white and filmy, so transparent he could see the faint line of an appendectomy scar along her flat belly. Springing off the table, she danced close to Rennick. On her forehead and upper lip there was a fine sheen of perspiration.

Rennick reached out suddenly and folded her into his arms. Her skin was hot as she pressed herself against him.

"You bitch," he said softly. "You god damn bitch!"

She nodded and pulled his head down with a strength that was surprising for a woman. She kissed him hard. Rennick put his hand behind her head and pressed his lips harder against hers, so hard that he knew he'd bruised her. His other hand sped down the curve of her back and slipped her panties off. He picked her up, cradled her black-stockinged legs for a moment in his arms, and then placed her on the floor. The phonograph record began to scratch but he knew he wasn't going to bother to shut it off. And he could tell by the things the girl was doing that she wasn't going to shut it off either.

Later, they sat at one of the mahogany tables and drank Cokes together. There was a pleased, happy expression on Vodka's face but the wildness was still in her green eyes.

"What about Georgetti?" said Rennick.

"To hell with Georgetti." Vodka ran her tongue over her even, white teeth. "Tell me about yourself."

"I'm just a guy looking for a guy and a gal."

"No, I mean your name and where you're from."

"Rennick. John Rennick."

She drained her Coke and set the bottle down on the polished table top. "Can I call you Johnny?"

"If you want. I'm not exactly the Johnny type."

"You're quite a man, Johnny." Vodka lit a cigarette,

handed it to him and lit one for herself. "What else can you do?"

"I'm in the oil business."

"You mean you're rich, too?"

Rennick shook his head. "I'm in the dirty end. I'm a derrick man. But right now I'm looking for a blonde."

"You think I'm the one?"

"Maybe. Can you play the piano and were you at the lounge at the Charlemagne last night?"

Vodka held up her hands and turned them over. "I only wish they could. They can't do nothing. Can't even wash dishes or sew a stitch."

"You might be lying," said Rennick. "I wouldn't blame you if you were. There's something about this deal that makes people keep their mouths shut."

"I've lied to lots of people," said Vodka and for a moment her green eyes weren't so restless. "But I wouldn't lie to you. I was at the Charlemagne last night but not in the lounge. My real name isn't Vodka—it's Mary. Mary Beth Engel and I'm no good, no good at all."

"How do you tie in with the Charlemagne and this," Rennick gestured, indicating the boat.

"I'm just a street walker that got promoted," said Vodka. "I guess you'd call me a yacht walker now."

"Are you Georgetti's girl?"

"Sometimes."

"You got any idea when he's going to get here tonight— or if he's coming at all."

Vodka shrugged. "He's already been here. Left about half an hour before you got here."

"Hell," said Rennick. He got up from the table. "Any idea where he was going?"

"He mentioned something about the Charlemagne."

"Hell," said Rennick again. "I can't go near the Charlemagne. But I guess I'll have to try."

As he moved away from the table, Vodka got up and caught his sleeve. "Can I go with you?"

"Why?" Rennick looked at her suspiciously.

"Take it easy, big boy." Vodka's green eyes were playful. "I'm on your side. I just want to go along because I like what you've got. A girl doesn't find much of that these days."

"Some other time," said Rennick. "I've got to play this one by myself for a while."

He opened the wardroom door and went out into the passageway. Standing in the doorway, Vodka watched him go.

"Will you be back?" she asked.

"Yeah," said Rennick, "I'm a hell of a bell ringer."

He heard her laugh softly as he went up the stairs to the upper deck. Crossing to the starboard side, he went down the ladder and got into the rowboat. He untied it and pushed off with long hard strokes of the oars. As he moved back toward the shore, he wondered how he could manage to get inside the hotel without being picked up. The cops had a theory that a killer always returned to the scene of the crime. And if they were still using it, the Charlemagne would be well patrolled even though it was nearly twenty-four hours since the cop was killed. Well it might not hurt to get close to the hotel and scout around.

When he was about a hundred yards from the quay, a shrill voice began to shout.

"Hey! I see him coming in! He's coming in!"

Rennick let go of the oars and twisted around on the smooth wooden seat. On the sidewalk above the small private piers, the kid in the yellow and blue T-shirt was jumping up and down and waving at somebody. He had a cap pistol in one hand and he was firing it rapidly. Small puffs of bluish smoke floated up around the street lamp behind him.

Rennick returned to the oars and began stroking. But the sound of an engine made him turn his head again. A black and white squad car came down the street from the direction in which the kid had waved. It stopped and doors flew open on both sides.

Without a second thought, Rennick went headlong over the side of the boat.

7

THE WATER HIT HIM WITH AN ICY SHOCK THAT NUMBED HIM
from the back of his neck to his heels. He clawed through it,
diving as deeply as he could and feeling the tight pressure in
his eardrums and against his throat. After the first shock
passed, he began to feel more at home. He knew he could
stay under for a full three minutes if he had to. He wrestled
with his shoes and got rid of them. His slacks came next.
When he kicked them off he had a feeling of regret as the
heavy .32 bore them downward. He needed that gun. He let
himself coast upward, his right hand stretched above his
head, feeling for the bottom of the rowboat. When his fingers
touched the rough incrustations of barnacles, he felt his way
along to the side. He allowed his face to break to the surface.
Quietly he sucked in a little air and looked around.

He'd come up about as he'd planned, behind the boat so
its shadow shielded him from the men ashore. Above the
sound of the water in his ears, he could hear hoarse voices
shouting orders and the kid's shrill piping. About seventy
feet away, the surface of the water was in the shadows between two of the quay lights. He submerged silently and began to stroke his way under water.

When he figured he'd traveled the seventy feet, he floated to the surface again, taking care to keep his hands and
arms under. He let his mouth and nose push above the surface an inch or so. He was glad there were no large waves
on the bay. Floating on his back for a moment, he filled his
lungs, noting with a small amount of professional satisfac-
tion that he'd come up in the shadows almost exactly where
he'd planned. Water blurred his eyes so he couldn't see
much of the shoreline. There was no way of knowing for sure
whether the cops had him spotted. Submerging again, he
swam seventy feet, a hundred and then another dozen or so
until his lungs were bursting. He eased to the surface again
and let his breath whistle out through his clenched teeth.
Again and again, he repeated the process of submerging,

67

swimming and resurfacing until he felt he'd swum at least two blocks parallel to the curve of the quay. Finally he allowed himself the pleasure of relaxing with his head completely out of the water. The shore was still a good hundred yards away. There was no sign of the two cops or the noisy kid with the cap pistol.

Rennick swam to shore with a speedy crawl that disturbed the surface only slightly. When he pulled himself up on a wooden float, the night air was cold against his dripping bare legs, much colder than the water had been. He shivered and wondered where he could get some dry clothing. It was a cinch that he couldn't travel far in his underwear, socks and water-logged sweater. He wished he hadn't been so hasty in getting rid of his slacks. Maybe he could find somebody's cast-offs in one of the alley garages across the street.

He walked along the float, transferred to some concrete steps and went up to the sidewalk. The street was deserted. There were no cars parked on it in this section and no pedestrians. Rennick crossed swiftly, went down a curved side street, cut through somebody's front yard and then through a gate to their back yard. As he padded along a concrete walk, he realized he was leaving a trail of water spots behind. If the cops were on the ball, they might be able to find where he left the bay and follow him. In a corner of the dark yard, he located a trash can. He dug out some old newspapers, dried off his legs and blotted some of the water out of the sweater. Then he passed through a rear gate into the alley. Before he'd gone a dozen feet, a car's headlights turned into the alley half a block ahead. Rennick ducked into the shadows along the side of a garage, wondering if it was the squad car.

The car came down the alley, purring along quietly in low gear. It passed him and Rennick breathed a little easier as he noticed it was a new Cadillac and not a squad car. He waited until the twin red tail lights twinkled at the far end of the alley and then he started walking again, trying to ignore the gravel that cut through his socks. Going from garage to garage, he tried three doors in succession and found them all locked. Headlights broke into the alley again and once more he ducked back, concealing himself this time in a recess between two garages.

It was the same Cadillac, moving slowly. This time it halted when it was but a few yards from Rennick's hiding place.

Somebody inside the car spoke, but the words were so muffled he couldn't understand what was being said.

The voice spoke again, louder this time. It was a woman's voice and it inquired clearly: "Rennick?"

He froze. Again the voice called his name, more insistently.

Rennick took a step forward so he could observe the car better. A girl was seated behind the wheel and the pale dash lights were strong enough to illuminate her profile. It was Josey.

Rennick stepped out into the alley. "Brother, am I glad to—"

He stopped. Because of the car's dim interior, he hadn't noticed the man who was seated at the far end of the front seat.

"It's all right," said Josey, "get in."

Rennick opened the back door and got in. Josey put the car in gear and they went slowly down the alley.

"There's a lap robe back there some place," said Josey. "Look on the floor."

Rennick probed around with his foot until he found it. He threw it across his legs.

They drove back to Rivo Alto Canal and then out to Second Street. Emil turned and looked back at Rennick.

"So you're Rennick," he said. "The man a hundred cops couldn't find. You must be good."

"How'd you find me?" said Rennick. "Sutro?"

Emil nodded. "We figured you were still in the neighborhood."

They rode on in silence for five minutes. Rennick felt uneasy. He wondered if he'd made a mistake in getting into the car. If it hadn't been for Josey, he wouldn't have risked it. She handled the big car with effortless ease. When they halted for a red light in Belmont Shore, she turned her head briefly and he got another good look at her. She was a remarkably beautiful girl. The strands of her yellow hair caught and held the glitter of all the thousand lights along the boulevard. The signal changed and she guided the Cadillac around a panel truck that had stalled in the intersection. They left Second and turned onto Ocean Boulevard.

"Where are we going?" said Rennick.

Emil turned slightly and looked back. "Does it matter?"

"I'll say it matters," said Rennick bluntly. "I don't know you two from Adam."

"You'll be safe enough," said Emil. "For a while at least."

"What do you mean—'a while'?"

"In this business," said Emil philosophically, "one never knows how long a good thing will last."

"I don't like double-talk," said Rennick. "If you've got something to say, say it or shut up."

Emil started to speak, changed his mind and turned so he was facing the windshield. Rennick wasn't sure but he thought he heard Josey laugh softly.

They drove a few more blocks down Ocean, approaching the tall, slim silhouette of the Charlemagne. It was an impressive building with a small, conservative yellow neon sign on the roof.

"Wait a minute," said Rennick. "I'm not going nowhere near the Charlemagne. Turn this buggy around and let me off somewhere else."

"We're not letting you off," said Emil. There was a nasty cut to his voice and Rennick decided his first impression of the man had been right.

"Well, damn it, I think you are!" Rennick tossed the robe aside and started to get up. He wasn't sure whether he ought to open the door and take his chances on the street or whether he ought to stay in the car and take a few pokes at Emil. The guy was asking for it.

"Take it easy, Rennick," said Josey. "We're not going to turn you in. We're going to make you a deal." The car was approaching one of the Charlemagne's curved driveways and she applied the brakes. "Get down on the floor and we'll have you upstairs in no time."

"What kind of a deal" said Rennick.

"You know you can trust me," said Josey. She stopped the car in the driveway and glanced back at him. Her large gray eyes were clear and direct. Rennick remembered last night—the hiding place in the closet and the key to the fire-escape gate that she'd given him.

70

"Go on," she said, "get down on the floor and throw the robe over you."

"I feel like a god damn rabbit," said Rennick. But he lay on the mat between the two seats and pulled the robe over his shoulders and head. The car rolled ahead slowly, made a turn and then seemed to go down a slight incline.

"Two cops are watching but I don't think they'll bother us," said Josey, raising her voice for Rennick's benefit.

After a moment, the Cadillac halted. A door opened and Rennick guessed that Emil had gotten out because of the way Josey spoke.

"Be careful with Emil," she said. "Play along with him and you'll be all right. Cross him and you'll be sorry."

"I don't like that bastard," said Rennick.

"I don't either," she said.

The car moved ahead again and halted after a few yards. Rennick heard heavy doors slam.

"Okay," said Josey, "you can get out now."

Draping the car robe over his shoulders, Rennick stepped out onto a concrete floor. He saw that they had driven into a cellar garage. It was a large garage with diagonal white lines painted on the floor as parking places for at least a hundred cars. But there was only one other car present besides the Cadillac.

"How come?" Rennick asked Josey, motioning at the emptiness. "I thought business was rushing."

"It's none of your business," said Emil, bolting the galvanized iron doors.

"One of these days you and me are going to tangle," said Rennick. He watched Emil take the ignition keys from the Cadillac.

"Suits me," said Emil.

The two men stood there a moment, looking one another over coldly. Rennick noted that Emil was as tall as he was and as thick in the shoulders—but there was a certain weakness around the man's smug mouth.

"Now, boys," said Josey, "time for that later . . ."

She led the way across the garage to a pair of elevator doors and punched the button on the wall. After an interval, the elevator arrived and they got in. It was a small, self-service model. Emil closed the doors and pushed the sixth-floor

71

button on the red panel. No one spoke while the elevator rose. When it stopped, they got out and crossed what looked like a small private hallway to a door that Emil opened with a key from a ring heavy with keys of all sizes and shapes.

Josey took off her jacket and tossed it across a lemon-colored chaise-longue. "Emil," she said, "be a good sport and get him some clothes to wear."

Emil shrugged and looked at Rennick. "I'll get you some clothes but I want you to understand one thing. Bringing you in wasn't my idea—it was Josey's. We'll talk it over and if I decide I don't like the way things look—out you go, understand?"

"He understands," said Josey. "Now get the clothes."

After Emil went into the bedroom, Josey stepped closer to Rennick. "You're supposed to know all about boats," she whispered. She passed him, went over to a sectional divan and picked up the afternoon paper.

It was a later edition than the one Rennick had seen in the morning. The headlines were so black he could read them from where he stood. He didn't like what they said.

Returning from the bedroom, Emil handed Rennick a pair of neatly pressed, brown gabardine slacks, yellow and brown Argyle socks, fresh underwear and a white shirt.

"Thanks," said Rennick. He went into the lavender-tile bathroom, washed, and ran a comb through his dark curly hair. He noticed that the skin was still raw around the metal band on his wrist. The clothes fit him well, although the slacks were a little large around the waist.

"How about a pair of shoes?" he asked when he returned to the living room.

"I guess we can manage," smiled Josey. She went into the bedroom and came back with a pair of sissy sport shoes that had blue canvas uppers and thick, yellow gum rubber soles.

"Well, I don't know—" Rennick raised his eyebrows.

"Beggars aren't choosers," said Josey. She winked at him.

"I think I just lost an argument," said Rennick, slipping the shoes on. They fit very well.

"Well, let's get going," declared Emil impatiently. "Let's go into the office."

He and Josey went through a side door into another room. Remaining behind for a moment, Rennick picked up the newspaper and scanned it. The busboy's death, emblazoned as the second murder at the Charlemagne in twelve hours, was the cause of all the headlines. There was a picture of the busboy on the front page. The picture made him look even younger, not much more than eighteen. He was smiling and his dark Mexican eyes were full of teen-age devilment.

Rennick swallowed. It was a hell of a thing to be responsible for something like that—and the fact that he hadn't meant to hit the boy that hard made no difference. The boy was just as dead as if he'd meant to.

"What's the hold-up?" growled Emil from the other room.

Rennick ignored him. He scanned the rest of the news articles, but there was no mention of the deaths of Laurette and Stanley. Which meant that somebody at the Charlemagne had a lot of power—either enough to dispose of two bodies or enough influence with the cops to keep the news out of the papers.

Dropping the paper onto a table, Rennick joined Josey and Emil in the other room. It was a large office with several dark green metal desks, filing cabinets and a handsome, rugged-looking wall vault. Emil was seated at the largest desk, toying with a fountain pen. Behind him was a huge white refrigerator, the only incongruous note in the office. Josey was seated on a brown leather divan, smoking a cigarette. Her handsome legs were crossed, but her skirt was pulled down demurely over her knees.

"We lost a man in our organization today," said Emil, waving Rennick to a chair. "I may give you his job, if I think you can fill it. I understand you were in the Navy."

"Marines," said Rennick. He wondered if the lost man Emil referred to was Stanley.

"Same thing." Emil unscrewed the cap on the fountain pen and then screwed it back on. "I understand you know something about boats."

"I can get along on a boat," said Rennick. He noticed that Josey's cool gray eyes were observing him carefully. "I was attached to the Navy for a while. We did a lot of work off of small boats."

"This one's not so small," said Emil. "I also understand
73

you got a medal for being pretty handy with guns. What kind of guns?"

"Any kind. Thompson. Reisling. Garand, .45 or 75 mm. —take your choice."

"Sounds pretty fair," said Emil. He turned in his swivel chair and opened the door on the refrigerator. "Anybody hungry?"

"I haven't eaten since breakfast," said Rennick.

Emil swung the refrigerator door all the way open, revealing shelves packed with foods in brightly labeled cans and jars. A satisfied smile worked across his plump mouth. "What do you like? Snail tidbits, caviar, *paté de foie gras,* slices of pickled watermelon, mangoes, hearts of palm, anchovies . . ." He reached up and pulled down a can with a green and gold label. "Let's try some of this."

After cutting the lid off with a can opener built into his desk, Emil opened a drawer and brought out a box of crackers. He opened another drawer and brought out a bottle of wine and three crystal glasses.

"La Dame Blanche," he declared. "Very fine white wine."

He poured the clear liquid carefully into the three glasses, handed one to Josey and one to Rennick. Then with a bone-handled carving knife he spread a brown paste from the can onto the crackers and distributed them to Josey and Rennick.

Rennick did not taste the wine. He bit into one of the crackers and was not particularly pleased with the flavor.

"What in the hell is this stuff?" he said.

"Goose livers," said Emil. "Three bucks a can."

"Tastes more like drippings off a candle," said Rennick, pushing the crackers aside. "What else have you got?"

Scowling, Emil picked up Rennick's crackers and ate them one by one. He finished his wine and turned back to the refrigerator. "You don't seem to realize how much this stuff costs," he grumbled. "I've got about $200 worth in this refrigerator alone." His eyes scanned the labels. "How about some rattlesnake? Very tender, packed by a man in Florida."

"Hell," said Rennick. "Haven't you got anything in my class, like say steak and potatoes?"

74

Emil snorted. "The trouble with you is you don't appreciate the finer things in life . . ." He turned to Josey. "How about you—or are you feeling high and mighty tonight, too?"

"I think I'd like some of those watermelon slices," said Josey.

Emil handed her a tall, narrow jar and she fished the green slices out by piercing them with a slender, silver cocktail fork. Once while she ate she glanced at Rennick and shook her head slightly. He didn't know whether it was a sign of warning or merely that she was displeased with the food.

"What about the deal?" Rennick inquired. He reached across the desk for some of the plain crackers and ate them dry.

"I'll think it over," said Emil. "If I decide to go through with it, I'll put you in charge of the boat. I'll hire a couple of flunkies to help you run it."

"Where do I take the boat and what'll I be doing with it?"

"Don't get ahead of yourself," said Emil. "I'll fill in the details—if I decide to sign you on."

"What's there in it for me?"

"In it for you?" Emil laughed sharply. "I won't turn you over to the cops—that's what's in it for you!"

"That's not enough." Rennick pushed his chair back and stood up. "What do I live on?"

Poking the blade of the knife into the can of goose livers, Emil licked it off delicately with this tongue. "I'll pay you a salary of a hundred a week and board and room."

"That's kid stuff," said Rennick. "A guy can make more than that sitting on his can around an oil derrick."

"A hundred and fifty," said Emil. From the refrigerator he took down several cans and a flat jar of caviar that was already open. "This is straight from Leningrad. And don't ask me how I happened to get hold of it. Want to try some?"

He looked at Rennick with hard, blue eyes, his lips pinched together in a plump line. It was obviously a challenge of some kind.

"I'd still rather have a hamburger," Rennick stared back coldly.

Emil rose from his chair.

75

"Now, Emil," said Josey, "he can't help it if he doesn't go for ritzy food."

The corner of Emil's mouth began to tremble. He walked around the desk to Josey. "Always taking anybody's side but mine?" he said. His voice was as brittle as thin glass.

Quite suddenly his hand whipped up and slapped her across the face. The blow was hard enough to throw her back against her chair and smear lipstick brightly across her cheek.

"You silly bastard!" said Rennick. "What do you think you're doing?"

As Rennick started after Emil, Emil whirled and picked up the bottle of wine. He threw it hard but inaccurately. It whistled past Rennick's shoulder and he heard it smash into a thousand bits on the filing cabinet behind him. Drops of wine and glass splinters spattered against the back of his shirt.

"All right," said Emil, "stop where you are and we'll forget the whole thing." Edging along the desk top, his fingers found the carving knife and closed around it.

"Drop it, Emil!" warned Rennick. From the corner of his eye, he saw Josey hurry across the room. He reached over the desk and picked up one of the heavy cans of food.

Uncertainty flickered in Emil's eyes. He started to back up. Then he raised the knife and started to approach Rennick.

Rennick threw the can. There was just enough room between the desk and the chair for him to get a good wind-up. He put all the arm he had into it and the can rifled across the desk and hit Emil squarely in the chest over the heart. The force of it knocked Emil backward and his shoulders slammed into the refrigerator. His face twisted with pain and shock and he began to cough. Again and again he coughed—deep racking coughs that left his shoulders shaking and turned his face red. He choked up, gasped for air and tried to spit.

Rennick went warily around the desk. He grabbed Emil's knife hand and twisted. Emil had a death grip on the blade and it took most of Rennick's strength to bend Emil's wrist until the knife dropped to the rug. Kicking the knife under the desk, he waited until Emil straightened up before he

76

smashed a fist into the fat mouth. Emil's knees bent inward and Rennick hit him again, high on the cheek his time, and Emil's head rocked back and hit the refrigerator door as he slid to the floor. He stayed on his knees for a second and then pitched forward flat on his face. Arms bent awkwardly under him, he lay there coughing and gasping for air.

Rennick rubbed his knuckles where they were skinned and looked around for Josey. She ran in suddenly from the other room, carrying a large black leather handbag which she opened as she ran. When she got to Rennick, a good-sized .32 automatic was clenched in her right hand.

She stopped and looked down at Emil. She turned to Rennick. "My God!" she said. "Now you've done it!"

"Slapping women around!" said Rennick. "What's the matter with that guy!"

"Plenty!" Josey's gray eyes were frightened. "And there must be something wrong with you, knocking him around like that!" She grabbed Rennick's arm. "I've got to get you out of here!"

Tugging at him, she started for the door.

8

AS THEY WENT INTO THE LIVING ROOM, RENNICK LIFTED the gun from Josey's fingers. She did not resist and he slipped it into the pocket of his slacks. She ran into the bedroom and returned in a moment with one of Emil's sport jackets, a chocolate brown model, which she tossed to Rennick. She snatched her own jacket off the chaise-longue and then they went quickly out into the hall and got into the small elevator.

They went down two floors and left the elevator, Josey leading the way along the corridor to Room 412. "You'll be all right here for a while," she said. "I don't think Emil knows I've got a key to this one."

They went inside and Josey closed the door and locked it. The room was completely bare of rugs and furnishings.

Rennick crossed to the single window and drew the shade. When he turned around, his eyes traveled briefly over the

77

bare hardwood floors and walls. "Somebody steal all the furniture?" he asked.

"There's a lot of crazy things going on in this hotel," said Josey.

"Yeah," said Rennick, "I've been noticing." He got his cigarettes out and offered Josey one. "You think it was smart to come here? Maybe I should've beat it while I had the chance."

"If I know Emil," said Josey, "half unconscious or not, he's on the phone right now telling the boys at all the doors to pick you up. If you wait a couple of hours you may get past them."

"Maybe," said Rennick.

He dragged smoke deeply into his lungs and watched Josey do the same. Again he found it hard to believe that this was the same girl who had clung to him in the darkness last night. Right now she looked like she'd stepped straight off a rotogravure society page. There was something expensive and well-bred about her that was more than just the cut of her clothes and the sleek way her blonde hair was drawn back to the gold barrette at the nape of her neck.

"And what are you staring at so boldly?" Josey asked.

Rennick looked into her cool gray eyes. "You. Do you mind?"

"No," she said, "I like it."

"I can't figure you out," he said.

"That makes us even . . ." Smiling, her red lips blew a stream of smoke up at him. "I don't know what it is about you. Maybe it's the knack you've got for rolling up in trouble, like a kitten rolling up in a ball of yarn."

Rennick laughed. "Nobody ever called me a kitten before. But you're damn right about the trouble."

"I just about had things fixed up for you with Emil," she said. "He could've done a lot for you. I don't think you realize he's the biggest man west of Chicago. In his field."

"I think he stinks," said Rennick.

"I'll admit he's no good," said Josey, "but you'd have been a lot safer on his boat a hundred miles off shore than dodging cops on shore. After all, you did lie to me last night, you know."

78

"What do you mean?"

"About the cop. You told me you didn't kill him."

Rennick nodded. "Yeah, I'm sorry about that."

"Sorry about killing the cop—or sorry you lied."

"Sorry I lied. As for the cop, that couldn't be helped. And if I could find the blonde who was at the piano—" He hesitated. "There was a blonde playing the piano at the Charlemagne when the cop was killed. I didn't get a good look at her. It couldn't have been you, could it?"

She shook her head. "I only wish it was."

"You wouldn't lie to me?"

Josey shook her head again. "Not to you."

"There are so damn many blondes in this deal," he said. "There's you and Vodka—"

"Quite a girl, that Vodka," said Josey.

"Yeah," said Rennick, remembering. "Quite a girl—but not in your class."

"Thank you," said Josey.

"And then there was Laurette," said Rennick. "Another blonde."

Josey looked down at the floor. "That was awful," she said slowly. "Poor Laurette . . ." She looked up at Rennick again. "How did you know about her? My god, you get around. Nobody's supposed to know about Laurette and Stanley."

"Any idea who did it?" he said. "You realize if it was Laurette who was at the piano, somebody killed her to keep her from telling what actually happened in the lounge? And there goes the only hope I had of getting the truth to the cops."

Josy dropped her cigarette on the floor and ground it out with her high-heeled slipper. "Laurette couldn't play the piano. The poor sweet kid—she couldn't do anything."

"That leaves you and Vodka," said Rennick. "And I'm eliminating you."

"So that leaves Vodka," said Josey. "She knows music but I don't know whether she plays the piano or not."

"It's up to me to find out." Rennick looked at his watch. "Nine-fifteen. I think I ought to be blowing out of here."

"You'd better wait at least an hour. After what you did to Emil he'll be crazy. He'll have his boys all over the place."

79

"The crazy bastard," said Rennick. "He had it coming."

Josey shook her head slowly. "If you knew Emil you never would have done it. He won't rest till he kills you."

"Kills me?" said Rennick. "Why would he want to stick his neck out like that?"

"In the first place you've hurt his pride by beating up on him. And that's the worst thing you could've done. In the second place, you've found out an awful lot about his organization in an awful short time."

"I don't know a thing compared to what you know," said Rennick. "For instance, what about this hotel?"

"Well," said Josey, "I really shouldn't tell you—but you look like a good listener. It's quite a long story." She sat on the floor, smoothed her skirt down around her long legs and leaned against the wall. Then she patted the waxed hardwood floor beside her. "Don't be so formal."

Rennick sat down and rested his shoulders against the wall. "I'm listening."

"Well, I can tell you how much the hotel's worth, almost exactly." Josey touched a scarlet-tipped finger to her temple. "About $1,210,000—I'm the corporation secretary and I keep the books."

"That's a fair piece of change," said Rennick. "Who owns the corporation?"

"Emil owns the corporation. He paid cash for it two years ago."

"Cash? Where'd he get that kind of money?"

"He's smart. Would you believe it—he started out with a delicatessen. That's why he's so crazy about those ritzy foods. He always wanted to have enough money to eat whatever he wanted. During the war, he branched out when money was easy to get. He opened first one house, then another."

"You mean girls?"

Josey nodded. "He made a fortune at it. After the war he sold out for a couple of million to some big shots from Los Angeles. He sat around vacationing for a few years, watching his other investments grow and then he bought the Charlemagne. He turned it into a corporation, Emil Groza Incorporated, with a board of directors, minutes and everything."

"And you're the secretary," said Rennick. He fished out his pack of cigarettes and they lit up again. "Somehow I didn't figure you for a secretary. Who are the directors?"

"I'm a director. So's Sutro and Vodka. Even Laurette and Stanley were directors. And there are a few other directors you haven't run into yet. But we're all just figure-heads. It's Emil's hotel and his corporation. He tells us how to vote and that's how we vote—"

There was a tap at the door. It was a single tap, light but urgent. Rennick looked at Josey.

"He can't know about this room " Josey whispered.

There was another tap at the door. A woman called anxiously: "Josey! Are you in there, Josey?"

"Who is it?" asked Josey.

"It's me—Chili!"

Rennick and Josey got up from the floor. Josey crossed over to the door and opened it. Chili came in and Josey locked the door behind her.

Under their dark lashes, Chili's eyes were frightened and her face was pale. Her dark curls were mussed and 'there was a rip in her orange-colored coat. She glanced quickly at Rennick, then at Josey.

"Who's he?"

"He's all right," said Josey. "What's the matter?"

Chili looked at Rennick again. "I seem to remember you from someplace . . ."

"This afternoon," said Rennick. "You were having a bout with a bottle."

A deep flush stole across Chili's tanned cheeks. "You! You're the one they were after!" She turned to Josey. "The police came to Georgetti's house. I don't know whether they caught Sutro or not. I went out through the bedroom window." She touched the tear in the sleeve of her coat. "I nearly broke my neck."

"I don't know what you're so worried about," said Josey. "The police won't find anything out there."

"They might." Chili took Josey aside and whispered something to her.

"Well, maybe," said Josey. "I guess you'd better find Emil and tell him. But don't tell him about seeing me and Rennick here."

"I won't." Chili went out, closing the door behind her.

"How come she knew you were down here?" said Rennick. "I thought this was your private hide-away."

Josey smiled. "Are you always so suspicious? Chili's all right. She's a director, too—but she's the only one I can trust. We help one another whenever we can. We used to be school teachers together, in San Diego."

"School teachers?" Rennick shook his head. "Don't kid me. You two don't look no more like teachers than I do."

"Shows you the difference a few months can make," said Josey. "Chili—her real name's Julia—taught the fourth grade and I had the room right next to her's, the fifth grade. I taught drawing, too."

Josey laughed suddenly. "Don't look so amazed! And if you're wondering how we transferred from arithmetic books to Cadillacs, well, it was easy. We got tired of being teachers, met Emil one night in a night club in San Diego—and here we are."

"That's quite a story," said Rennick.

"It's not just a story. It's the truth—but you don't have to believe it if you don't want to." Her fingers took Rennick's and squeezed them gently. "You know, all the men I've met —Emil, Sutro, Stanley, and some others—I haven't liked any of them. But you, John—"

Her large gray eyes looked up at him softly and he noticed a pulse beat fluttering in her white throat.

"What about me?" he asked.

"You're tall and so, well, sure of yourself. I like you, John. I like you a lot. And there's a devil in me—"

She moved into his arms and he held her tightly for a long moment, feeling how small and slender she was, feeling her warm ear against his cheek and the nearness of her breathing. When he kissed her he wondered how he ever could have gone for Vodka. There was no comparison. Where Vodka had been sarcastic and artificial, Josey was real and honest, emotionally honest. He kissed her again and they held one another so closely he could feel the curve of her thigh against his own. His hand moved under her jacket to the hollow at the small of her back, finding pleasure in the warmth of her clothing.

"I can't help it, darling," she whispered. She pulled his

82

head down and kissed him again, her mouth moving under his, making him feel all the soft, moist textures of her lips and the smooth hardness of her teeth.

"You're a hell of a fine woman," said Rennick hoarsely. "A hell of a fine woman!"

"That's the nicest thing anybody ever said to a school teacher!" She kissed him once more and then withdrew slowly from his arms. "But I'm afraid we have to be practical . . ."

"What's that got to do with it?" Rennick pulled her into his arms again and kissed her until she gasped.

"But we do!" she said. She touched his cheek with her fingers and then drew away. "There'll be time later—later we'll have all the time we want, but you'll never get away if we—"

"I don't like to quit when I'm ahead," Rennick growled.

"Now you're making noises like a wolf." Josey smiled. She smoothed down her skirt and buttoned her jacket.

"When'll I see you again?" he demanded.

"What do you mean 'again'?" said Josey. "I'm going with you."

"With me?" said Rennick. "Are you kidding? What about Emil?"

Josey's gray eyes grew darker. "He's slapped me around for the last time."

"Now you're talking," said Rennick. "Brother, let's get out of here!"

"Not if you're going to treat me like a brother!" She smiled up at him and Rennick grinned back.

"You're the sexiest brother I ever had," he said.

He waited while she dug into her large black handbag. "I like to see you like this," she said, taking out a cigarette case, comb and crumpled Kleenexes. "You've been so serious."

"I've had a lot to be serious about," said Rennick.

"Damn!" said Josey. "I was afraid of that."

"What's the matter?"

"The car keys. They must be up in my room."

"You mean the Cadillac?"

"No. Emil's men would never let us get it out of the

basement. I've got another car on a parking lot across the street. But we'll have to go up and get the keys."

Josey closed her purse. Rennick went to the door, looked out and saw that the corridor was empty. They walked along the hall to the staircase and went quietly but swiftly up the carpeted steps. They met no one and after five minutes reached the top floor. Josey unlocked a door and they stepped into a large suite. Long, golden drapes flowed down from the ceiling and the lime green shag rug was as cushiony as a golf course. The overstuffed chairs and the long low divan were beautifully made and looked as if they'd cost a fortune.

"You won't get this kind of stuff if you stick with me," said Rennick. "You'll be lucky if there's a dirty mattress to sleep on."

"That's the way I want it," said Josey. From a closet, she brought out a small, blonde leather traveling case. "I guess. I might as well bring along a few things."

She opened the case and set it on a table. It already held cosmetics and a traveling alarm clock. She added some paraphernalia off the table, including a magnifying glass and some small wooden-handled cutting tools.

"What's all this stuff for?" Rennick picked up one of the chisels and felt its sharp edge.

"Just some things I use for wood-cuts." Josey placed a box of stationery on the table and started for the bedroom. "I used to teach wood-cutting in San Diego. Wait'll I get a nightgown or two and I'll be right with you."

A moment after she went into the bedroom, she called out to him and he could tell by the break in her voice that something was wrong.

Rennick strode into the bedroom and although it had been totally dark last night he recognized it as the bedroom in which he had first met Josey. Now she stood rigidly over in the center of the room, her hand pressed hard against her cheek, her eyes staring at the girl who sat so uncomfortably in the comfortable-looking, frieze-upholstered chair.

Rennick crossed the room slowly and looked down at the girl. It was Vodka and she was dead. Her hands still clenched the arm rests and her legs were twisted against the chair legs as though she had made a terrific effort to stand

84

after the bullet had torn into her breast. The blood was not especially noticeable because the material of her tight-fitting wool dress was a deep wine-color. Her head had fallen forward so her chin rested on her breast and her straight, bright yellow hair—fixed in its capricious horsetail—hung at a grotesque angle.

"I guess I won't have to ask her whether she was the one at the piano," said Rennick. He felt sick to his stomach. A few hours ago, Vodka had been happy as a kid, dancing on the table aboard the boat, making love to him while her green eyes laughed over her Coke bottle.

"It's awful!" Josey turned away and covered her face with her hands.

"Damn 'em!" said Rennick. "This damn dirty stinking place and the people in it!"

He strode back into the living room, slammed the traveling case shut and picked Josey's handbag up from the table. When he returned to the bedroom, Josey was sitting on one of the twin beds, her shoulders quivering uncontrollably.

"It could've been me," she whispered. "It could just as easily have been me . . ."

"It could still be you." Rennick took her hand and pulled her up from the bed. "Come on, make tracks."

Shoving open the window, he stepped out on the fire escape. Josey followed and they went down the metal steps through the darkness until the iron gate barred their progress.

"Damn it!" said Rennick. "What kind of a fool would put a gate on a fire escape? Have you got a key?"

Josey nodded and opened her purse. As she handed him a ring of keys, she dropped them. Rennick made a wild grab, missed and the keys struck the iron grillwork with a clang that Rennick was sure could be heard in the alley far below. He waited, expecting to hear the sound of the keys bouncing from landing to landing all the way down the fire escape. But there was no further noise. Dropping to his knees, he felt around until he found them. They were wedged in the open space between two of the iron bars that formed the grillwork.

"That's a break," he whispered. He opened the small padlock and after they passed through the gate he locked it

85

again. Pausing a moment, he leaned on the railing and looked down through the darkness, studying as much of the fire escape as he could see. It seemed to be deserted—and if it wasn't, well, that was the chance they would have to take.

He handed the traveling case to Josey and got the .32 out of his pocket. He kept it in his hand as they moved downward.

When they reached the short ladder that hung over the alley, Rennick dropped off first. Josey tossed the traveling case and her handbag and he caught them and set them down on the paving. She hung for a moment from the bottom rung, her long legs swaying above him, and then she let go. She dropped into his arms and he could feel the young firmness of her hips as he set her down.

Picking up the traveling case, he started down the alley toward the beach.

Josey tugged at his sleeve. "The car's in the lot across the street!"

"I know," said Rennick. "And Emil and his boys probably do, too."

He led the way along the side of the hotel for half a block until they came to the sand. It was hard packed and they were able to walk across it without much difficulty. They walked southward until they could see the white foam and boiling waterfalls of the surf and hear the boom of the water against the sand. Then they turned to the right and walked west toward the downtown section of the city.

After they walked about two blocks, they left the beach and went up a flight of stairs to Ocean Boulevard. Rennick stopped in front of a cubby-hole newsstand.

"I don't like to send you alone," he said, "but I guess it's the best way. What kind of a car is it?"

"A club coupé. A green Studebaker."

"Okay. And for god's sake, Josey, cheer up. It wasn't your fault Vodka got killed."

Under the harsh lights from the newsstand, her face was pale. "I know—but if I'd been there I might have been able to—"

"You couldn't have done anything." He gripped her arm. "Nobody could of. Now get going."

Josey nodded. She walked away from him down the sidewalk and Rennick turned and went into the newsstand. Holding the traveling case under his arm, he picked up a picture magazine and flipped through the pages. After a moment, he noticed two men come into the narrow space between the racks of brightly colored magazines. One wore the dark uniform of a cop and the revolver in his hip holster looked ugly and efficient. Rennick felt the muscles in the back of his legs grow tense. Under his breath, he cursed himself for allowing the two men to block the way to the entrance. The place was so narrow he wouldn't be able to pass inconspicuously around them. The cop picked up a detective magazine and with a critical eye studied an illustration of two policemen making a silent approach on a hoodlum in front of an open safe. Rennick realized that he was holding his own magazine so tightly his fingers were creasing the pages. The cop put down his magazine, moved closer to Rennick and picked up a girly magazine. He stood so close to Rennick that his black leather holster almost rubbed against the .32 in the pocket of Rennick's slacks.

Moving back a step, Rennick raised his magazine and glanced over the top edge past the cop's shoulder out to the street. He knew it was too soon for Josey to be there yet—but he hoped she was.

She wasn't. He had an instinctive desire to rush from the place, put as much space as possible between himself and the cop. But he forced himself to stand and glance quietly at the pictures in the magazine. When he looked up again, a car was double-parked out in the street. It was a black and white squad car. He swallowed dryly, feeling a pressure in his ear-drums as his throat muscles rebelled against swallowing when there was no saliva to swallow. He wondered if the squad car meant they had him spotted. It wasn't logical that so many cops would be in one place without a good reason.

From the corner of his eye, he watched the cop and the squad car. He saw a green Studebaker coupé cruise slowly past the squad car and continue on down the street. The cop turned suddenly. His hand went toward his holster and Rennick dropped his own hand down near the pocket of his slacks. The cop's hand went past the holster into his pocket and brought out a coin. He paid for a magazine, went out to the sidewalk and then into the street. Opening the right-hand door on the squad car, he got in. The car drove away.

Rennick waited a full minute before going out to the curb. In a few moments, Josey drove up in the new green Studebaker and Rennick got in beside her.

"My god!" Josey said. "That car! I was sure they had you!"

"It wasn't so bad." Rennick dabbed at the sweat on his forehead. "All I had to do was wait."

They drove on several blocks. "You can put the case in the back if you want," said Josey.

He knelt on the seat, leaned over and lowered the traveling case to the floor in the back. As he straightened up, he noticed the gleam of reflected street lights on a familiar metal surface. He switched on the dome light and confirmed his suspicions. There was a slot machine on the floor behind the seat. And there was no doubt that it was the same slot machine because the sawed-off chain and the mate to the steel ring on his wrist were still attached to the scroll-work near the coin slot.

9

"I'LL BE DAMNED!" SAID RENNICK, STILL KNEELING ON THE seat. "How did it get back there?"

"What?"

"The slot machine."

Josey immediately parked the car near a vacant lot and got up beside him on the seat. She shook her head. "Why would they put it back there?"

"All I know is Sutro was damn interested in finding it," said Rennick. "Who else uses this car besides you?"

"They all do. Emil uses it. And Sutro. And Chili does too, sometimes."

Rennick switched off the dome light. "Sutro said he wanted to put it in a joint somewhere in town. Sounded fishy to me. Well, there's no sense worrying about it now."

He walked around the car and got in behind the wheel.

Josey snuggled close to him and he put his arm around her. They drove down Atlantic Avenue and turned west on Highway 101. He had no particular destination in mind—and he didn't care. All that mattered was that they were putting miles between themselves and the Charlemagne.

"Who do you think did it?" Josey asked, after a long silence.

"Did what?"

"Killed Vodka."

"Your guess is as good as mine. I can't even guess why she was killed—or why Laurette and Stanley were killed. The whole thing's a mess. Even that poor kid, the busboy—"

He hesitated. He felt Josey turn and knew she was looking at him.

"What about the busboy?" she asked.

"Nothing," he said.

In silence they drove on through Harbor City, Torrance, Redondo Beach, Manhattan Beach and other ocean towns. At Santa Monica, they stopped for gas. When the attendant stepped up to collect, Rennick remembered that he'd lost his billfold in the bay along with his slacks.

"I'll handle it," said Josey. She handed Rennick a twenty-dollar bill from her purse.

"First time I ever had a woman pay my way," he said. "I don't like it."

He gave the change to Josey but she handed the bills back to him. "Cheer up, grouchy," she smiled. "You can pay me back later if you think you have to."

"I will," he said.

"What you need is something to eat," said Josey. "I've always believed that the way to a man's heart is through his stomach—even if I had to get somebody else to do the cooking."

"Okay," grinned Rennick, "you win. I haven't had anything to eat since breakfast."

"What about those delicious goose livers?"

"Yeah . . ." Rennick pulled her closer and rubbed his cheek gently against hers. "Best damn goose livers I ever ate. Remind me to sling a can of 'em at Emil next time I see him."

Josey was silent for a moment. "I hope you won't see him ever again," she said. She paused. "Ever."

They stopped for dinner at a large restaurant with candle-lit tables near picture windows overlooking the ocean. Their waiter was a small dark-haired man in a white jacket.

"A cocktail before dinner, folks?" he asked, handing them menus.

"Yes," said Josey. "I'll have a Manhat—" She glanced at Rennick. "No, thanks. Just dinner for us, please."

"You didn't have to do that," said Rennick, after the waiter had left.

"But I didn't want a drink," said Josey. "I really didn't."

"Thanks," said Rennick. He covered her slim white hand with his large rough one.

They ate New-York-cut steaks, discovering that they both liked their meat medium rare. The rest of the meal consisted of baked potatoes with cheese sauce and chopped onions, succotash, dark pumpernickel bread, large tossed green salads, pumpkin pie, and coffee. Rennick was glad to see Josey eat everything on her plate, including the potato skin.

"I like a gal with a big appetite," he said. Feeling comfortably full, he put down his fork.

"I'll probably get fat," Josey's gray eyes twinkled at him.

"You better not." He reached over the table and took her hands in his. He looked at her and he felt as warm inside as if he'd had two or three drinks. He looked at her for a long time, admiring the way the candlelight touched the waves in her bright yellow hair, admiring the perfect formations of her ears and her full red lips. He looked at her slim throat and her broad shoulders and the firm, rising lines of her breasts under the tweed of her jacket.

"I like you, Josey," he said suddenly.

"And I like you, John. I may even . . ."

"May even what?"

She smiled a mysterious feminine smile. "Later . . ."

When they returned to the car, Rennick drove back to the highway and they continued north past the hills of Malibu and the gaudy neon of occasional gas stations and motels. Rennick felt calm and rested. The only reminder of the day's previous hectic hours was the weight of the .32 in the pocket of his slacks. He tried to dismiss the nagging

90

thought from his mind that Emil might have turned the license number of the coupé over to the police and that they might run into a road-block at any time. He wasn't sure that he'd done the right thing by running away. It deprived him of any chance of tracking down the blonde, provided she was still alive—and that meant the killing of the cop would remain on the books as murder.

"Why so quiet?" asked Josey.

Rennick reached out and pulled her closer. "Just thinking. And sometimes it's not good for a man."

"What were you thinking about?"

"The cop. And the way it all happened . . ."

"Would it help any to tell me about it?" She leaned her head against his shoulder.

"Maybe," said Rennick. He paused. "I know it sounds crazy but the whole thing really started in a billiard room about a week ago down on Pico Street near the harbor. A couple of guys and me finished a few games and we were sitting at the bar having sandwiches and beer. The other guys were having the beer. The bartender was drunk, real blind drunk, and kept trying to overcharge us a couple of bucks. First thing we knew, he grabbed a pistol from a drawer under the cash register and started waving it at us. I was standing the closest to him and I made a grab and got hold of the gun."

"You could've got yourself killed," said Josey. She shuddered against him.

"It would've saved me a lot of trouble if I had." Rennick lit a cigarette with the lighter from the dashboard. "I made the mistake of hanging onto the pistol when we left. I couldn't see any sense in giving it back to that crazy bartender. When we got out on the street, I put it in my pocket while the other two guys kidded me about being a hero. We hadn't gone half a block before the cop stopped us. He'd been at the bar and saw the whole thing. He was a plainclothes guy and he sent my two buddies on their way. He took the pistol and ordered me into his car. We talked I don't know how long, a half hour or so, and then he told me he was letting me off with a warning, but that if he wanted to he could run me in for assault, theft for stealing the pistol, and for carrying a concealed weapon. I don't know how many charges he had against me. Well, he let me go, all right."

"And then?" asked Josey.

"About two nights later he turned up at my place. He had a deal for me. I was supposed to go to the Charlemagne and make myself a few bucks and if I didn't play ball he'd run me in on the gun charges. Well, he had me. I knew I couldn't get any place trying to report him to his chief or anybody because I had no witnesses. And I might as well admit the idea of making a few bucks appealed to me. So I turned up at the Charlemagne a couple of hours after midnight expecting to meet Georgetti, who was going to explain what I had to do. Only he never showed. Instead Sutro and Stanley turned up and took me up to the cocktail lounge. There was nobody else there but those two guys and me and the blonde playing the piano by herself over in the corner. It was dim over there and I never did get a good look at her—not that there was ever time. In about five shakes the cop came in and I didn't like the look on his face. He pulled out a gun. It was the same gun I'd taken away from the bartender. Nobody said anything but I knew I was some kind of a patsy. There was something in the way Sutro and Stanley looked at the cop. The cop tossed the pistol to Sutro but I made a reach for it. Soon as I caught it, the cop got out another gun, his own gun, and opened up on me. I mean it was no accident, no misunderstanding. He missed me—and I did the only thing I could do, the only thing anybody could do with a gun in his hand. I shot him in the shoulder and it spun him around. He grabbed a lamp and started to fall. I figured that was the end of it but he fired at me again and I couldn't just stand there and let him do that. I shot him once more. I shot him right beside the ear . . ."

Rennick lapsed into silence. The coupé rushed on through the night, the wind rustling softly at the open wind-wings, the wheels whining keenly against the pavement. Neon signs appeared as bright pin-heads in the distance, grew into giant splashes of color and then abruptly vanished. Occasionally, the highway dipped down beside the beach and they glimpsed the surf.

"I think you did the right thing," Josey said, after a whole. "There was nothing else you could do."

"I don't know," said Rennick. "If it had been the first time, maybe."

"What do you mean 'the first time'?"

"I'd rather not talk about it, Josey."

"I understand, darling." She rubbed her cheek against his arm. "What happened afterwards?"

Rennick lit another cigarette. "They got hold of me, Sutro and Stanley. We had a hell of a time smashing up a couple more lamps and then all the lights went out. They knocked me down and yanked the gun out of my hand, but they made damn sure my prints stayed on. I never saw anybody as glad as Sutro was about the whole thing. I didn't know what he was glad about, I still don't. While they were busy holding me down, the blonde skipped out. I think Stanley made a grab for her, maybe that's how her purse got knocked into the mix-up, but anyway she got out of there." He paused and glanced at Josey. "While I think of it—have you got any idea what they wanted me up there for in the first place?"

"I heard some talk," she said. "I heard that the cop was asking for a bigger cut and threatened to ruin the whole deal. I think Emil was going to kill him and set it up so it looked like you did it while trying to rob the hotel safe. Only things got out of hand."

"The bastards," said Rennick. "They sure had me picked out." He drove on in silence for a few moments. "Well, anyway, Sutro took the cop's handcuffs and then they took me up on the roof, over to that part where the roof garden is with the chairs and umbrellas. They hooked me up to that damn slot machine because they wanted to make sure the cops got me, but they didn't want to stick around. I heard them say Georgetti was going to come and see that everything was set up just the way they wanted the cops to find me. In the meantime, somebody else called the cops—I figure it was the blonde—so Sutro and Stanley had to beat it the hell out of there."

"And a little later you came crashing into my room," said Josey. "And I'm glad you did."

"You saved my neck. More than once—and I'll never forget it, Josey."

"I like your neck, darling." She reached up and touched

93

the oval of steel that pinched his right wrist. "But I don't think so much of your taste in jewelry. Does it hurt?"

Rennick shook his head. "I'm getting sort of attached to it."

"That's a very bad joke," laughed Josey. "But I won't hold it against you."

They drove on through the night. After a while, Josey looked at her watch and yawned. "It's nearly two—don't you think we ought to stop someplace?"

"Got any idea where we're at?"

"Could be somewhere around Santa Barbara," said Josey. "I don't know." She pointed to the sign of a large motel built on a hillside near the highway. "That looks like a nice place."

Rennick turned the coupé into the asphalt driveway and drove up the incline to the motel office. Like the other units, it was a low, California ranch-style building constructed of simulated adobe with exaggerated eaves. Rennick went up to the door and rang the bell. After he rang it a second time, he heard activity inside and in a few moments the door was opened by a tousled-haired man whose pajama top was stuffed into a pair of trousers that weren't completely buttoned.

"Guess I'm too sound a sleeper for this job," he said. "Come on in."

Rennick walked over to a small varnished counter that was built into one end of the living room. He signed a fictitious name on the registry slip and put San Francisco down as his home town.

"Come very far?" the man asked.

"Pretty far," said Rennick. He scowled at the blank line calling for his license number and was tempted to put down a phony number.

"Can't remember your license?" asked the man. "Most people can't. I'll copy it off in the morning."

Rennick nodded and laid Josey's ten-dollar bill on the counter. The man gave him back four dollars and a key and Rennick returned to the coupé. He felt uneasy about the license number. If the police were broadcasting it or running it in any papers, the motel owner was just the kind of a sharp character who would spot it. On the other hand, maybe Emil hadn't turned the number over to the cops. He decided not to worry about it.

He drove to the far end of the lot and parked in front of No. 18. Josey got her traveling case from the back seat and they went inside.

"I think I'm going to like it here," she said after Rennick switched on the lamps.

He locked the door and looked around. It was a large room with a blonde, hardwood television set, blonde dressers and a wine-colored rug that had a minimum number of spots and ash burns. There were large mirrors on the walls and a freshly laundered yellow chenille spread on the Hollywood-style bed.

Josey stretched her arms over her head and went up on tiptoe. "I feel so free. No more Emil." She smiled up at Rennick. "How do you feel, John?"

"Good," he said. "Damn good." He took her hand. She let him hold it a moment, then pulled away.

"I'll be right back," she said. "You won't go away?"

"What kind of a fool do you take me for?"

"We're both fools." Smiling, she slipped off her jacket, tossed it over a chair and went into the bathroom.

Rennick took off his coat and hung it in the closet. From the pocket of his slacks, he took out the .32 he'd taken from Josey back at the hotel and examined it. It was a compact little weapon with the appearance of never having been fired. He slipped out the clip and inspected the bullets. There were six, all slightly corroded. He wiped them off, tested the firing mechanism and then replaced the clip. He put the gun in the pocket of his coat and closed the closet door.

In a moment, however, he opened the door again and took the coat out. He laid it across the top of one of the dressers, the pocket with the gun face up. It didn't pay to take chances.

He went over to a pink plaid chair, sat down and lit a cigarette. He wondered if it would always be this way—hiding out, keeping a gun handy for the hour or day when they might find him. He wished he hadn't left town so suddenly after finding Vodka. There was a good chance she wasn't the

95

blonde. And he'd left before finding Georgetti—the one man who might know who the blonde was.

Josey came out of the bathroom. She walked slowly to the center of the room and Rennick got up. He noticed that she'd put on fresh lipstick and brushed her yellow hair till it gleamed. He put his arms around her and kissed her on the side of the neck.

She trembled against him. "I feel so good, John," she whispered. "So good—and so naughty. Just like when I was fourteen."

"I'll bet you were a doll when you were fourteen."

"It was behind the lockers in junior high school—and I felt very wicked."

"Wicked?" said Rennick. "What in the hell were you up to?"

"My first kiss," whispered Josey. "This big tall kid grabbed me and I couldn't get away—so I let him do it and I thought it would be wonderful. A girl's first kiss is supposed to be, you know."

"And it wasn't?"

"No," laughed Josey, "he'd been eating licorice—and I hate licorice!"

"I haven't been eating licorice," said Rennick. He pulled her to him and kissed her hard. He could feel the freshness of her lipstick and he liked the sweet taste of it. He kissed her again, more gently this time, and then he stepped away from her.

"Walk for me, Josey. I like the watch you walk."

Smiling at him, she walked over toward the bed. Rennick's eyes never left her. She carried herself erectly, but not in the exaggerated way of a model. He watched the quiet movement of her thighs against the material of her skirt. Then he stepped quickly over to her and kissed her, long and hard.

"Kiss me again," she said.

He did and he knew he'd never felt this way before in his life.

He fumbled with the buttons at the back of her yellow blouse. The top one wouldn't unbutton. He tugged too hard and it popped off, bouncing under the bed.

"Damn it," he said.

96

"Kiss me," she said, closing her eyes.

Rennick kissed her again. He removed her blouse and swiftly unzippered her skirt. She wore no slip.

"Walk for me again?" he asked.

She stepped away and walked across the room from him. Her breasts pushed up beautifully against the snow-white nylon brassiere. Her panties were cut very briefly and they were a cool lime green with the word Friday repeated several times in embroidery down each thigh.

"Friday?" said Rennick. "I don't get it."

Josey winked at him. "Silly. These are the ones I wear on Friday. I wear blue ones on Saturday, white ones on Sunday and yellow ones, I think, on Monday . . ."

Hands on her hips, she turned around slowly. "Like them?"

"Damned pretty," said Rennick. "And no school teacher ever had legs like those. Turn around again."

She turned slowly, taking small steps with her high-heeled pumps. He admired her slim waist and the pretty hollow along her spine just above the edge of the green panties.

"So I'm not a school teacher?" Her gray eyes smiled at him impishly. "To find the circumference of a circle multiply the diameter by 3.1416. To find the area of a circle multiply the square of the diameter by .7854. The square root of 8 is 2.828 and sedimentary rocks are formed out of sediment deposited in water. Magellan sailed around the world in—"

"In a canoe," said Rennick, "and you're definitely a school teacher."

"Do you mind?"

"Hell no, I like the idea." He caught her in his arms again and kissed her solidly.

Josey leaned back and looked up at him. "You're wonderful, John. I knew it the moment I saw you last night. You're big and you're strong—but you're gentle, too, John, and a woman appreciates that. Especially now—you haven't rushed me. You've played with me and a woman likes to play . . ."

She clamped her warm hands around his neck and pulled his head down. Her lips brushed quickly against his and then

97

her fingers flew down the front of his white shirt, unbuttoning it.

"Take me now, John," she whispered. "Take me."

She was wild and she was wonderful. She was a slim animal with sharp teeth and claws and she was a perfumed woman with gentle lips and warm breath. Her face, her whole body, grew hot as fire. Her fingernails raked the tough skin of his shoulders while her eyelashes, long and soft, caressed his cheek. He had never for an instant believed it could be like this. He had never known anything like this. She had promised everything and she gave everything and more.

10

IN THE MORNING, HE WOKE SLOWLY. HE LAY THERE FOR A long moment without moving, remembering how it had been, and then he turned over to touch her. But Josey's side of the bed was empty. Rennick got up and looked into the bathroom. She wasn't there. He looked at his watch. It was nine o'clock.

"Josey?" he called. He opened the closet and then stepped quickly to his coat that was slung over the dresser. The .32 was still in the pocket.

He noticed that her clothes were gone. Swiftly he put on his trousers, shirt, and shoes and opened the front door. He stepped outside just as the green Studebaker coupé came down the asphalt driveway.

"Hello, handsome," said Josey. She crossed her arms on the wheel and looked out at him, her gray eyes warm and pleased.

"Where in the hell have you been?" said Rennick.

"You not only sound like a bear—" she smiled—"but you even look like one with all those black whiskers."

"Sorry," he said. "You gave me kind of a scare, running off like that."

"You were such a sleepy-head." Josey opened the car door and stepped out with a small cardboard box and some bulging paper bags. "I thought I could get back before you woke up."

She walked inside and placed her bundles on the bed. From one bag she drew a new brass razor, some blades and shaving cream, a toothbrush—and a small hacksaw with a fine sharp blade.

She handed the objects to him, went up on tip-toe and kissed his cheek. "Scratchy! Now you go in and clean up while I fix breakfast."

Rennick went into the bathroom, washed and shaved, moving the razor gingerly around the small cuts inflicted by Sutro and Stanley. When he returned to the bedroom, Josey had steaming coffee waiting for him which had been poured into paper cups from a new thermos bottle. There were bananas and Rice Krispies in paper plates and cream in a cardboard carton.

"Did I tell you how wonderful you were last night?" Josey asked as they ate.

"I believe you mentioned something like that."

"Don't be so modest," she laughed.

"You were pretty wonderful yourself," he said. He watched her drink from her paper cup, admiring the curve of her wrist and the clean line of her throat as she tilted her head back.

They finished breakfast, lit cigarettes and Rennick picked up the saw and went to work on the thin ring around his wrist. The blade's small teeth were sharp. In fifteen minutes he'd removed the steel.

"Damn it, I'm glad to get rid of that," he said, rubbing his wrist.

"A lovely way to start the day," said Josey, dropping the pieces of steel into the waste basket. "And it's a beautiful morning, besides—California sunshine all over the place."

Rennick nodded.

"Don't look so glum, darling." She squeezed his hand. "We're in Ventura and it's a wonderful little town. White houses on a hill. Palm trees and an ocean so blue it must have fallen from the sky."

"Sounds awful good, Josey. But I can't help thinking about all the things that happened yesterday. The more miles we put on the speedometer the better I'll feel."

Josey shook her head. "This is a good town, John. And I think it's a lucky town. Come here, I want to show you something."

Rennick followed her out the door to the small porch. Josey pointed to a green hill behind which rose the dark steel towers of a dozen oil derricks.

"What did I tell you?" said Josey. "Isn't this a lucky town?"

"A bunch of new rigs and it looks like they're running a lot of pipe." He turned and looked at her. "Are you suggesting maybe I ought to get a job?"

She nodded, her eyes sparkling.

He looked at the derricks again, and considered the possibilities. They had driven only about a hundred miles up the coast and he would much rather continue up to Oregon or Washington or maybe Canada. On the other hand, the cops might be patrolling all highways with orders to look for a certain green Studebaker coupé. They could leave the car behind and go by bus or train but that might be more hazardous. Cops never found it very difficult to check passengers in a train or bus station. If he dropped out of sight in a small town, got a job, changed his name—they might never find him, even if he was only a hundred miles away. Lots of guys did it every year and were never caught.

"What do you think, darling?"

"I don't know," he said. "I need a little time to figure the odds."

"You're the boss," said Josey. She led him back to the bedroom and closed the door. "And just to show you I'm serious I want you to take care of something for me."

She opened her purse and took out a packet of currency which she handed to him. "I want you to handle it. Pay all the bills and everything and then after you go to work you can pay me back if you want."

Rennick riffled through the money. There were at least a hundred twenties in the stack, at least two thousand dollars.

"Where in the hell did you get all this?"

She shrugged. "Emil. He pays his secretaries very well. And I was a director, too."

"But two thousand bucks. No secretary gets paid in a damn big chunk like this!"

100

Josey put her arms around his neck and laughed at him. "There you go scowling and swearing again. It's very simple, John. I saved Emil at least a hundred thousand dollars on his taxes and he was grateful, that's all."

"Damned grateful."

"You're jealous and it's very becoming." She sighed. "But I suppose I'd better explain. You noticed how there were never any people on the upper floors of the Charlemagne, no cars in the garage?"

Rennick nodded.

"Well, only a few rooms on the lower floors were ever rented. That left all the other rooms vacant—a couple of hundred of them. At night, Chili and I and Sutro and the rest went around lighting a few of the lights on the upper floors so all the windows wouldn't be dark and the place wouldn't look completely deserted. The idea is that in a year Emil can claim a terrific loss—a legitimate loss of two hundred thousand dollars and it'll all be there in the books for the income tax men to inspect. Nice and legitimate."

"Emil hasn't got rocks in his head. What's the gimmick, what's the catch to it?"

"On his other deals, Emil makes two hundred thousand—and that about offsets his losses on the hotel so he doesn't have to pay a tax."

"What other deals?"

Josey shrugged. "A few houses and girls. He didn't sell all his places. And he's got a finger in a new kind of bookie deal that beats the law."

"But so what?" said Rennick. "That still doesn't explain—" He hesitated. "Wait a minute—I think I see it. He makes more dough on the girls and bookie deal than he puts down on his form. But because he's listed all those deals on his form, the income tax boys figure he's playing ball—and besides there's no way for them to itemize everything. What does he do—keep two sets of books on the houses and bookie deal?"

"Yes. Altogether he figures to clear about another two hundred thousand. And that doesn't count what he thinks he'll make with the boat, and he's counting on the boat deal to be the biggest and the best."

"For god's sakes," said Rennick, "I have to hand it to the guy, as much as I hate his guts. He's smart."

"Well, I like that!" Josey frowned and pretended to be hurt, but there was a twinkle in her eyes. "Let's give credit where credit is due, and, besides, I thought you wanted to know why he paid me the two thousand dollars."

"So it was you who figured it out." Rennick shook his head slowly. "You're an amazing woman, Josey."

"Not bad for a school teacher?"

"Not bad at all," he said. "And on the boat deal Emil figures to make even more. What's he going to do—run a gambling ship out at the three-mile limit?"

"I don't know," said Josey. "Emil let me in on nearly everything else but the boat's his pride and joy. I think he would have told me later but he took pains to keep me in the dark up to now."

Rennick placed his hands gently on her shoulders and looked into her eyes. "You wouldn't kid me, would you, Josey?" He tried to keep his tone light.

She shook her head, her gray eyes hurt. "No, John, I wouldn't kid you . . ."

"Don't take it so hard." Rennick placed a finger under her chin and tilted her head upward. "It's just that I have a tough time understanding why a pretty little doll like you would unload a guy like Emil, with all his greenbacks and Cadillacs, for a guy like me who can't give you nothing but headaches."

"Maybe it's something else you've got . . ." Josey spoke softly and put her arms around his middle. "Whatever it is, I like it." She began to rub her hip slowly against his thigh. Reaching up, she loosened the top button on his shirt, and then stepped quickly away, moving to the other side of the room. She whisked off her blouse and unzipped her skirt. It slid down her slim legs to the floor and she gave it a skillful kick that lifted it to the chair.

She turned around and looked at him. "Good morning, John . . ."

"Damn it," he said, "you're beautiful." He noticed that she wore yellow panties with the words Monday embroidered on the thigh. "Whatever happened to Saturday and Sunday?"

102

"I was in such a rush last night I only brought along Monday." She began to walk toward him. "Do you mind?"

"Does that mean I have to wait until Monday?"

"Don't be crazy . . ." She came into his arms and kissed him, pressing the points of her breasts against his chest. She kissed him in rapid succession on the chin, on his throat and beside his ear. "I felt this way about you the first time I saw you, John . . ." Her voice was low and throaty, almost hoarse.

"When you winked at me in the coffee shop?" He grabbed a handful of her yellow hair, pulled her head back and rubbed his jaw gently against her cheek.

"No, the night before . . ." She kissed him full on the lips and the wonderful urgency of her drove deep inside him sending his own desire soaring to the heights. He held her tightly, ignoring a small corner of his brain that sent him a warning. *The night before?* His fingertips played with the smooth skin of her back, unhitched her bra and swept down to the yellow panties.

Later, they dressed and went outdoors to sit side by side in canvas chairs beside a table and red beach umbrella in the motel's patio. The sun was hot and relaxing. Eyes closed, Rennick lay back in his chair and drowsed, feeling perspiration gather on his forehead as the sun climbed higher and the heat of its rays increased. He held Josey's hand quietly in his own and they remained silent for many minutes, enjoying the nearness of one another. It had been a long time since Rennick had known such quiet. Before there had always been the howl of the draw-works and the ring of heavy pipe against the steel of the derrick. Even his room had never been this quiet—if there wasn't the groan of a streetcar making the turn at American and Ocean, there was the rattle of a trash truck in the alley behind.

"Wouldn't it be wonderful?" asked Josey.

"Wouldn' what be wonderful?"

"If it could always be like this," she said. "No rushing around, no running away, no fear that the next time the door opens there'll be trouble . . ."

Rennick sat up, suddenly uncomfortable.

103

"What's the matter, darling?" Josey looked at him anxiously.

"Nothing," said Rennick. "You just brought me back to earth, that's all. And I guess there'll always be something to bring me back to earth."

"What do you mean?"

He squeezed her fingers. "It's nothing to get excited about. It's just that every time I think things are going to be all right, something comes along and wrecks everything. It was that way in the Marines and it's been that way since I got out. Just as I was beginning to think I was normal, I killed that cop. The bullet got him right beside his ear. And now I'll never be able to see a gun, or even see the word gun printed in the papers without remembering how that cop looked as he went down. I figured I'd paid the price for what happened the first time—I haven't touched one drop since it happened. But then the same thing happens again—and this time I was sober, cold sober. It's been this way ever since I was a kid. Everything I ever touched turned to crap, everything—"

"Don't, darling," said Josey. "Don't torture yourself." She got out of her chair, leaned over him and kissed his forehead. Her lips were cool.

"Anyway, I don't believe you," she said. "I know you must've done some very fine things. What about the medal? How many men ever won the Medal of Honor?"

Rennick sat up straight and looked at her suspiciously. "How did you know about that?"

"Sutro told me."

"And I suppose he told you how I carried the clipping around, too," Rennick's mouth twisted bitterly. "And how I yanked it out of my wallet and started bragging about what a big god damn hero I was "

"No, darling, he didn't." She smiled. "But must you glare at me like that?"

Rennick dropped back into his reclining position. He lowered his voice. "I just want you to know that I carried that clipping around for one reason. It was a reminder—a reminder of what happened on Iwo Jima. Every time I bought a pack of cigarettes or paid for a meal—every time I looked in my wallet—it was a reminder of what happened

104

on that god damn rotten island. It was a reminder of the god damn awful thing I did to get that medal. And even though the clipping and that wallet are on the bottom of the bay, I'll think about it every time I open any wallet that I ever own—"

"Take it easy, darling." Josey's hand covered his own where it gripped the chair's arm-rest. "Maybe it would help if you told me about it. I know it can't be as bad as you think it is."

"It wouldn't help, Josey." Rennick laid his head back against the canvas. "It wouldn't help me forget anything. Neither Iwo, nor the cop nor—"

"What?" said Josey.

"Nothing," said Rennick.

He closed his eyes and tried to sweep all those other thoughts from his mind, tried to think only about the soothing heat of the sunshine and the breeze that was blowing in from the ocean and the way it felt to have Josey at his side, a warm, wonderful woman who was worried about him, concerned about him.

But after a few minutes he sat up again, restless and uncomfortable. "I can't get those things off my mind. Like Laurette and Vodka. I keep wondering who killed them and why they were killed and wondering whether there's a connection."

Rennick paused. Then he turned in his chair and looked at Josey. "You know the whole bunch. Who do you think did it? Do you think it was Emil?"

She shook her head. "No, I don't think so. They were both Emil's girls—and he was mean to them sometimes but I don't think he killed them."

"You mean they were from one of his houses?"

"Yes. He decided he wanted them for himself and took them to the hotel. Vodka was very high-priced goods. She told me once she'd gotten as high as $150 at the swanky house out on Country Club Drive. I don't know where he found poor little Laurette—but I think she was happier at the Charlemagne than she'd ever been before."

"She was always that way?" asked Rennick. He tapped his temple.

Josey nodded. "And I know what else you're thinking—
105

you're thinking that I was one of Emil's girls, too, and you're wondering how much I made a night . . ." Turning away, she looked out across the fields at the green hills in the distance. Her chin was high and the line of her throat was exquisite.

Rennick touched her shoulder gently. "I won't say I haven't thought about it. After all, he did have a pretty free run of your bedroom. But you're with me now, Josey, and everything that happened before, well, it's just like it didn't happen . . ."

When Josey turned and looked at him again, her gray eyes were moist. With her fingertips she wiped at the corners. "I know you won't believe me; I don't expect you to believe me—but I was never more than his secretary. He tried, god how many times he tried, but I never let him . . . I knew it was wrong, John, living in the hotel like that, and if that should be the thing that comes between us, I'll never . . ."

Her voice trailed off. She looked at him as if she was afraid he would get up from his chair, walk down the highway and never return.

"I'm not very good at this kind of talk," said Rennick quietly. He reached out and took her hand again. "I believe you, Josey. I guess it's because I want to believe you."

"Thank God, darling!" She held his hand tightly and though she blinked rapidly she failed to hold back the tears. Glittering brightly in the sunlight, they clung to her lashes and then ran down her cheeks. She wiped at them furiously with the back of her hand. "I'm such a fool, darling. Such a fool, but I can't help it."

"Don't try," said Rennick.

Holding hands like a pair of newlyweds, they remained side by side in the canvas chairs for a long while. They spoke very little and when they did speak it was about little things —a foreign-make car that was parked at the next motel unit, a fat man in gaudy shorts who came, dripping wet, from the beach; a tired old woman in worn slippers who trudged from unit to unit changing the linen and making the beds.

Later, Rennick and Josey got into the green Studebaker and drove a mile down the highway to have lunch at a sprawling ranch-house restaurant. They left the car on a

106

parking lot and took a table for two in a pleasant alcove near a window. They didn't pay much attention to the people who were dining around them and Rennick looked up in surprise when two men and two girls came up to their table.

"Hello, Josey," said one the girls. "Having a good time?" She looked at Rennick. "How are you, good-looking?"

It took Rennick a moment to recognize her. When he realized it was Chili, the slim brunette who'd been at the Charlemagne, he felt a sudden stab of danger. He shot a glance at Josey. She'd grown pale and upset her glass of water.

"Come on, Josey," said Chili. "Let's make a party of it. Let's all sit at one table."

Josey didn't move. There was an awkward silence during which Rennick sized up the three others who were with Chili. The two men wore flowered silk sport shirts that hung sloppily down over their trousers. They were small dark men with snapping black eyes. They were almost identical in height and appearance, except that one wore heavy-rimmed glasses. The sport shirts did not conceal the fact that they looked like a pair of Chicago hoods, although as far as Rennick could tell they seemed unarmed. He cursed himself for leaving the .32 at the motel and for parking the Studebaker right next to the highway. It was Emil's car and he should have known how easy it would be for Emil's mugs to spot it.

"What do you want?" asked Josey.

"We want some lunch," said Chili. "Come on, don't be so stiff-necked about it!"

"Did Emil send you?" asked Josey.

"Emil?" Chili smiled mysteriously. "Who's Emil?" She turned to the two men. "Did you ever hear of anybody by the name of Emil?"

Both men shook their heads.

Chili turned to the blonde. "Ever hear of anybody called Emil?"

The blonde didn't know what to say. She looked in blue-eyed confusion first at Chili and then at the two men. Then for protection she took the arm of the man with glasses. She didn't say anything.

"Well, come on," said Chili. "Are you going to join us?"

107

Glancing at Rennick, Josey shrugged. They pushed their chairs back and followed Chili and the others over to a large table near the bar. After a round of drinks was ordered, Chili made the introductions.

"These are the Womack brothers," she said, indicating the two men, "Alfred and Mike."

"Call me Michael," said the one wearing the heavy-framed glasses. His small dark eyes blinked nervously at Rennick.

"And this is Rosemary," said Chili, introducing the blonde. "Lately of Country Club Drive . . ."

Michael put his arm around the blonde. "Not any more she ain't. She's my girl now and that's the way it's going to be. Right, Rosemary?"

The blonde nodded uncomfortably.

When the drinks were served, Rennick did not touch the Martini that had been ordered for him. Josey merely sipped at hers.

Alfred pushed the glass toward Rennick. "Come on, buddy, drink up—it'll make you feel better."

"I don't want it," said Rennick.

"Oh?" said Alfred. He stood up, his mouth twisting. "Too good to drink with us, is that it?"

"I don't drink," said Rennick. He reached out, grabbed Alfred's thin arm and his thick fingers squeezed slowly until he could feel the bones and tendons squash together. "Understand?"

He set Alfred back down in his chair with a small crash and released him.

Across the table, Michael took his arm from around the blonde. He got a small gun out of his pocket and laid it near his glass, covering most of it with his hand so people at other tables wouldn't notice.

"Let's keep this all friendly," he said, looking at Rennick.

11

"SURE," SAID ALFRED, "LET'S KEEP IT FRIENDY." RUBBING
his arm, he gave Rennick a weak grin. "Let me tell you
about the time in Cleveland when me and a pal ran into
two fairies. They were real dolls, both of 'em—perfume and
everything, and they even wore lady's wrist watches. You'll
die laughing when I tell you what me and my buddy done
to 'em!"

Alfred kept talking, but Rennick ignored him. He watched
Michael pocket the little pistol and keep his hand on the
pocket.

After a moment, Rennick transferred his glance briefly to
Rosemary. Small and well-built, she had tremendous blue
eyes and blonde hair cut short and fluffy. There was just a
hint of darkness at the roots where her hair was parted. She
had beautifully kept hands and wore a large diamond on the
ring finger of her right hand. He remembered Chili mention-
ing that Rosemary had worked out at the swanky house on
Country Club Drive. Since it was one of Emil's houses, that
meant Rosemary knew Emil and anybody who knew Emil
must've turned up sooner or later at the Charlemagne. He
wondered if Rosemary could've been the blonde at the piano.
Several times she glanced at him from across the table, but
there was no hint of previous acquaintanceship in her glance.

"So we tied 'em down," Alfred was saying, "and then we
started pouring the turpentine. Boy, you never—"

"Shut up!" Rennick told him abruptly. He looked across
the table at Michael. "What did Emil send you punks here
for?"

Michael spread his hands. "Nothing. A few drinks and a
good time maybe. What else?"

"Go someplace else and have a good time!"

"Listen, tough guy . . ." Michael's hand moved toward
his pocket.

Rennick stood up, his hands turning into fists. "You touch
that gun and I'll jerk you across the table so fast you'll think

you got hit by a ten-ton truck!" He glared at Alfred and the two other girls. "Now get out of here, all of you. Beat it!"

Michael's hand darted into his pocket and at the same time Rennick started to lunge toward him.

"No, John!" Josey caught his arm with both hands and hung on, twisting him around.

By the time Rennick tore loose, Michael had the gun out and leveled at Rennick's belly. Behind the heavy-framed glasses, Michael's eyes were shiny black with hatred. He stayed in his chair, concealing the small gun from the other diners in the room by covering it with both hands and keeping it below the edge of the table.

Rennick remained standing, his hands slowly opening and closing at his sides. He clenched his teeth and fought to keep his anger controlled.

"I'm sorry, John," Josey whispered, "but you might've gotten shot . . ."

Rennick said nothing. He watched Michael, waiting for the little man's next move.

"I think the party's over," said Michael. "Too bad . . ." He nodded at Rennick. "You and your doll lead the way out. But first you pay for the drinks."

Rennick slowly laid one of Josey's twenties on the table beside his untouched glass.

"Skip the change," said Michael. "Let's go."

Rennick walked between the small tables in the bar and then out through the main dining room. He knew Josey was at his side but he refused to look at her. He heard the others walking behind them.

"Please don't be angry." Josey caught his hand.

"It's okay," said Rennick. "It's just that I'm so god damn mad and can't do a thing about it!"

When they got outside, Michael directed them across the parking lot to a silver-gray Cadillac sedan. Rennick and Josey were told to get into the back. Chili also got into the back, pulling down one of the jump seats. She looked at Rennick and shrugged. The other three got in front—Alfred behind the steering wheel and Rosemary in the middle. Michael sat halfway turned around so he could keep the pistol aimed at Rennick.

"Okay," Michael told Alfred.

Alfred punched the chrome starter button and put the Cadillac in gear. The big car moved quietly across the parking lot, drawing to a halt beside the green Studebaker. Leaving the motor idling, Alfred got out. He opened the door on the coupé, leaned inside and came back carrying the slot machine. The load was almost too much for him. With a grunt, he dropped the machine on the thick carpeted floorboards in front of Josey.

Josey gave Rennick a puzzled glance. They didn't speak.

Returning to the wheel, Alfred drove the big car onto the highway. They sped north briefly and then Alfred turned into the motel where Josey and Rennick were staying. There was no hesitation or doubt—it was obvious that they knew exactly where they were going.

Alfred parked the Cadillac in front of No. 18. Michael ordered Rennick and Josey out.

"Open the door," he told Rennick.

After Rennick unlocked it, Alfred went in while the others waited outside. In a moment, he returned carrying Rennick's .32.

"The only one I could find," he announced.

"Okay," said Michael. He nodded at Rennick and Josey. "You two get inside and take things easy for a while. We'll let you know when you're wanted."

As Rennick and Josey went in, the door was slammed behind them. Rennick swore and prowled around angrily. He went into the bathroom and confirmed what he already knew to be true. There was no bathroom window, just a small screened vent in the ceiling. Returning to the bedroom, he stood in front of the single window and watched Michael who was leaning against the fender of the Cadillac talking to Alfred.

"God damn it!" Rennick pounded his fist against his palm. "I'd like to knock their god damn heads together. How in the hell did those little bastards ever find us?"

Josey sat on the bed, her shoulders slumping. "I don't know . . ."

"Who are they?" asked Rennick.

"They're two of Emil's men."

Rennick swore again. "I knew we shouldn't have stopped. We should've drove all night!"

"It's my fault . . ." Josey's voice was small and tortured.

"It's all right." Sitting down beside her, Rennick put his arm around her. "We'll swing it all right. It looks to me like Emil sent a couple of boys to do a man's job."

Josey shook her head. "Don't be fooled by how little they are. They're mean. Emil paid a lot of money to get them to come out from Cleveland."

"They don't look so tough." He got up from the bed and walked over to the window. "How in the hell did they know the slot machine was in the coupé?"

"Maybe they helped Emil put it there," said Josey. "I heard Emil mention once that he was going to drive it out to the boat."

"I don't understand why they're so interested in it." Rennick realized he was pacing nervously up and down the floor. He went over and sat in the chair by the window so he could watch Michael and Alfred. "You got any idea why?"

Josey shook her head. "I used to think—"

The door opened and Michael came in. "We want to talk to you, Josey. Get outside."

Rennick got up from the chair. "Where she goes, I go."

"Not this time." Michael kept the gun trained on Rennick's shirt front. "Just stand easy . . ."

The little man held the gun with practised ease. He was calm and very sure of himself.

Rennick remained standing in front of the chair. He felt completely powerless as he watched Michael escort Josey outside.

"You stay right where you are, friend." Michael started to swing the door shut. "You put one foot outside and Alfred will put a little hole in your guts."

"I'm going to break your god damn neck!" said Rennick as the door slammed.

Through the window, he watched Michael take Josey to the motel unit directly across the driveway, No. 17. Apparently the others had rented it because they took Josey inside. Only Alfred remained outdoors, leaning against the polished gray fender of the Cadillac.

Rennick shoved the chair closer to the window so he could watch the door of No. 17 more easily. His throat was dry and for some reason felt swollen when he swallowed. He wished he'd taken that Martini at lunch. Getting out his pack, he lit a cigarette and puffed at it furiously, his lips pinching the end until it flattened and bits of tobacco scattered across his tongue.

Fifteen minutes passed. Half an hour. He went to the bathroom and drank a glass of water. When he returned to the chair, things hadn't changed. The venetian blind was still drawn shut on No. 17. For the tenth time in ten minutes, he tried to guess what they were doing to her. He told himself that if they touched one of the yellow hairs on her head, he'd kill them. He'd kill all of them.

When he sat down again, he noticed that his fingers were trembling. He was surprised. All the things that had happened the last couple of days—running from the cops, risking his neck a dozen different ways—and not once had he trembled. But now . . .

He held up his right hand again. The fingers were unmistakably shaking. He put his hands in his pockets. And quite suddenly he knew why. He'd known many women before in his life. There'd been others like Vodka, women whom he'd known briefly and forgotten. But there'd never been one like Josey. He'd known that the instant he'd recognized her voice in the coffee shop and admired the line of her throat in the mirror. She was prettier than any of the others he'd known. Her figure was certainly the most beautiful. And he knew it all, from the tiny roller-skating scar on her left ankle to the light brown mole between her breasts. But it was more than knowing her that way, as wonderful, as fiercely wonderful as that was. It was more than the confident manner with which she wore her clothes. It was more than the curve of her mouth and the way she held a cigarette. It was more than the way her large gray eyes grew more gray when she swore, or was scared or was laughing. He'd never thought about these things in a woman before. They'd never been important before. No woman had ever been important to him before.

Touching a match to another cigarette, Rennick sucked the smoke in deeply. He looked at his watch. Nearly an hour had passed. He told himself again that as much as he wanted to he couldn't risk a one-man attack on No. 17. They might kill Josey before he could break the door down.

113

He stayed in the chair and kept his eyes on the door of No. 17.

When it finally opened and Josey came out, led by Michael, Rennick strode to his own door and yanked it open. Instantly Alfred sprang to attention, the gun making a pointed bulge in his pocket.

"Back inside, buddy!" he commanded.

"Shut your god damn yap!" Rennick stood in the doorway and waited as Josey hurried across the driveway.

She shut the door and ran into his arms. Her shoulders were trembling and she clung to him for a long moment, breathing hard. When she looked at him, her face was pale but her eyes were shining.

"Oh, John! I think it's going to be all right!"

"It took long enough, for God's sake!"

"I couldn't rush them, darling!" She kissed him and then danced a few steps over to the dresser.

"What do you mean—rush them?" Rennick felt himself frowning. He had expected her to be frightened and upset. Instead, she returned happy and vibrant, brimming over with enthusiasm.

She touched a lipstick to her mouth and then sat on the bed and patted the yellow chenille spread. "Sit down, darling, and I'll tell you!"

Rennick sat down beside her. He lit another cigarette, handed it to her, and lit one for himself.

"Emil sent them up to find us, all right," said Josey. "I guess they followed us last night, or weren't very far behind, from what Michael says. But the thing is, Michael's sore at Emil because of Rosemary. For a couple of weeks Michael's been after Emil to let him take Rosemary out of the place on Country Club Drive. Emil wouldn't go for it. So when Emil finds out Michael brought her along on this trip, there's going to be a big blow-up."

"What the hell's that got to do with us?"

"Everything. Michael and Alfred have orders to take us back to Emil. But because of Rosemary, Michael doesn't want to go back and Alfred does whatever his brother says. So it's a double-cross. Instead of taking us back to the Charlemagne, Michael wants us to team up and take over the boat when it gets near Santa Rosa Island."

114

"What does he mean take over the boat?"

"He says he's sure Emil will only have three or four men on the boat. He wants to rent a small boat and make a raid on Emil—he figures we'll have surprise on our side and they'll quit in a hurry."

Rennick got up from the bed and looked thoughtfully out the window. Michael and Alfred were sitting in the Cadillac. They waved at him.

"I wouldn't trust those two little bastards as far as I can throw them!" He went back and sat beside her. "Do you mean it, Josey? Would you team up with a couple of crumbs like that?"

"It's not just them," said Josey. "Chili's in on it, too, and I trust Chili. Besides, if we don't, they'll take us back to Emil and you know what that means."

Rennick lit another cigarette. "I don't like it, Josey. I don't like any of it. What's supposed to be on the boat that they're so all-fired anxious to get?"

Josey frowned. "That's the part I don't like. They claim they don't know."

"Brother!" Rennick laughed bitterly. "That settles it!"

"I know what you're thinking." Josey got up from the bed and began to walk slowly up and down the space between the bed and the dresser. "But I also know that I tried to find out what Emil was going to load on the boat—and I couldn't. When he wants to, Emil can be more close-mouthed than anybody." She walked over to the bed and looked down at Rennick, her gray eyes dark and serious. "But I know this much, John. Whatever is on the boat, it's worth plenty. I got that much out of Emil."

"Don't look so serious," said Rennick. He pulled her down so she was sitting beside him on the bed. Then he put his arm around her and lowered her gently until she was lying diagonally across the spread, her yellow hair fanning out brightly. She looked up at him expectantly, her mouth open, the fresh red lipstick glistening. He kissed her gently, then harder. He raised his head and looked at her. Then he ran his finger down her cheek, tracing an imaginary line that went down the smooth skin of her throat, across the soft roundness of her left breast and back up to her cheek.

"Josey," he said, his voice suddenly husky, "I've seen too

115

much of trouble, all kinds of trouble, to ask for any more. I think if anything happened to you, I'd go crazy. Besides, what do Michael and Alfred need us for—why don't they forget about us and pull their deal alone? Then they wouldn't have to split."

"They can't handle it," said Josey. "They don't know the first thing about boats. They need you to run the little boat out to the islands and then run the big one after we take over."

Rennick rolled over and looked up thoughtfully at the ceiling. "I don't like the way they've got everything figured out. It's too pat."

"Well, I don't like the way you're acting." Josey got up suddenly from the bed and walked over to the chair. "I spent a whole hour over there agreeing that you'd help, that you'd run the boat and everything. And now you start talking like you're afraid."

Rennick got up slowly from the bed. "What did you say?"

"I said you talk like you're afraid."

Rennick went over to her. He grabbed the back of the chair and spun it around so she was facing him. "Nobody talks like that about me!" His voice was taut and low. "Not even you, Josey!"

Her gray eyes were blazing as she jumped to her feet. But quite suddenly her expression softened and he knew somehow that it was because of the way he was looking at her. But he couldn't help it. He felt the muscle knotting up along his jaw.

"I'm sorry, John," she said softly. "I didn't mean it that way. I know you're not afraid. Of course, you're not afraid."

But the anger in him was still mounting and he couldn't rein it in. "The whole deal stinks, that's all! We'd be fools to trust those two little punks! You can't trust nobody in a deal like this. You can't trust Rosemary, you can't trust Chili. And sometimes I think I can't even trust you!"

She looked at him for a moment without reaction. And then she went white. He knew he shouldn't have said it, but now that he had he wanted to say the rest of it and hear her deny it.

"Yeah, that's what I said. And I'll give you a for instance. You said you went for me the first time you saw me and

116

when I asked if it was at the coffee shop you said no, it was the night before. Only you couldn't have seen me the night before because the lights were short-circuited and your room was dark. So you know where that leaves me?"

"No . . ." The pulse in her throat was fluttering.

"It leaves me thinking this. You saw me all right that night. You saw me in the cocktail lounge. You were the blonde at the piano when the cop got killed!"

Now that he'd said it all, the anger went out of him like an exhausted flame. He stood there looking at her, towering over her, waiting for her to deny it and hoping he'd be able to believe her if she did.

Josey's hand went to her throat. When she spoke, her voice was almost a whisper. Her words were cold and as impersonal as if she were reading a timetable. "I was never in the lounge . . . I was standing in the hall with Georgetti when you got out of the elevator and first went into the lounge. That's when I saw you—and then I went to my room and stayed there . . ."

She turned away from him and walked swiftly into the bathroom. She slammed the door but it did not latch.

Rennick hesitated. Then he went to the door, opened it and went in.

She was leaning against the wall, her face buried in the fluffy white towel that hung from the chrome rack. Her shoulders were quivering.

When he tried to turn her gently around, she fought him, twisting and turning to keep out of his grasp.

"I believe you, Josey," he said. He knew he should say something more, but he didn't know what to say or how to say it.

Ignoring him, she kept her face buried in the towel.

"I believe you, damn it!" he said. He caught her shoulder and turned her around. Her face was pink and drenched with tears and her lipstick was smeared.

She put her arms tightly around his chest and pressed her face against him so fiercely that he could feel the warm dampness of her tears on his shirt. He held her until her shoulders stopped shaking.

"It wouldn't matter if I didn't love you, John . . ." she
117

said. "But I do—I love you so much that you can hurt me, you can hurt me more than you'll ever know . . ."

She looked up at him and there was so much pain in her eyes that he kissed her quickly, tasting the sweet brine of the tears that had run down to her mouth.

"I wasn't going to tell you," she said. "I didn't think you wanted me to love you. And if you don't love me, it's all right. I'll—"

"But I do," Rennick said hoarsely. "I guess I found out when they had you over there talking to you. If they'd laid a finger on you, I'd of smashed them to bits!"

"Oh, my darling, my darling!" She pulled his head down and for a long moment rubbed her damp cheek tenderly against his.

"I'm getting you all wet," she whispered after a while. "Here." She took the towel and patted his face with it.

"You said you were standing in the hall with Georgetti," said Rennick. "I've heard plenty about that guy. Who is he?"

"Emil's right hand. Whenever Emil's got some sort of a dirty job to do, Georgetti does it. Like that deal with you and the cop at the hotel, Georgetti—"

Her voice broke off as the bathroom door opened. It slammed into Rennick's shoulders and when he turned around he found himself looking at Alfred. The .32 was grasped snugly in the little man's hand.

"Christ's sake," said Alfred. "Here we've got a deal cooking and you two stand around billing and cooing." He jerked his arm toward the bedroom. "Let's get back to business."

Rennick considered making a play for the gun, but decided against it. In the small room, there was too good a chance that Josey might get hurt. Silently, he followed Alfred and Josey out to the bedroom. It was already crowded—Chili was sitting on the bed and Michael and Rosemary were standing near the dresser. Instead of carrying a gun, Michael led a bulky paper bag.

"Is it a deal?" asked Michael. He looked at Josey.

"It's up to John," said Josey. "If he says it's all right, we'll do it. If he says no, we don't." She took her purse off the bed and began to repair her smeared lipstick.

118

"What about it?" said Michael. This time he looked at Rennick.

"As far as I'm concerned you're just a couple of small-punk bastards," said Rennick.

"And maybe I agree with you." Michael smiled uneasily. "But that's neither here nor there. Now what about the deal?"

"I'm thinking about it," said Rennick.

"I guess that's your privilege." Michael's voice was steady but his eyes, behind the thick lenses, were nervous. He set the paper bag down on the dresser. "In the meantime let's have some refreshments."

From the bag, he took a tall bottle of bourbon, some glass tumblers that still bore price tabs and a jar full of cracked ice. While he opened the bottle, Rosemary put the ice in the glasses.

"Rosemary," said Rennick, bluntly, "were you at the Charlemagne after midnight the night before last?"

Rosemary dropped a jagged triangle of ice into a glass. She turned slowly and looked at Rennick. "I don't think so. The night before last?"

"You sure you weren't the blonde at the piano?"

"Music's not my specialty," she said simply. Her expression was quite frank. "My specialty's men, big or—"

"All right, all right," Michael nudged her with his elbow. "Try to forget your specialty for a while."

Rosemary shrugged and turned back to the glasses. Rennick watched her for a moment, wondering if she'd been lying. From the corner of his eye, he noticed something pass in front of the window but he didn't pay it any attention until the front door flew open.

Emil came in followed by Sutro and a third man Rennick didn't recognize. They carried guns.

Emil's face was pale and sweaty but there was a faint smile on his fat lips. "The big guy goes first," he said. "And Josey next . . ."

Sutro and the other man began to shoot and somebody screamed.

12

Rennick threw himself at Josey. His shoulder hit her hip-high and they went down together, with Rosemary who had somehow gotten in the way. They rolled together on the rug, a tangle of legs and arms, while the small bedroom reverberated with blasts of fire. Trying to get to his feet, Rennick saw Michael standing calmly by the dresser firing a pistol from the pocket of his slacks. Behind him, in the bathroom doorway, Alfred was pouring lead from the .32. The third man, the one with the crew-cut hair and the bow-tie, scowled and flopped forward onto his face. Sutro clamped a hand over his arm where it was leaking red and backed out the door, followed by Emil. They fired more shots as they ran to a dark blue convertible that was idling nearby. Its spinning rear tires left long black marks on the asphalt as it took off down the driveway.

The bedroom became quiet. Wisps of bluish gun smoke drifted idly over the bed and then, caught by a sudden draft, were sucked out the door.

Rennick crawled over to Josey who was struggling to untangle her legs from Rosemary's. He felt a stab of horror when he saw the blood smears on Josey's yellow blouse.

"My god!" he said. Then he saw that the blood wasn't hers. It was blood that had poured from the hole in Rosemary's breast. Rosemary lay on her back, her neck twisted awkwardly, her lips parted, one hand pressing against her dress where the bullet had drilled accurately into her heart. Michael dropped to his knee beside her and touched her cheek. He swore softly.

"She didn't want to come," he said, as if he were speaking to himself. "She was afraid to come because of Emil." He looked at Josey, but there was neither malice nor condemnation in his glance. "It was meant for you. It ought to be you laying there instead of her . . ."

Rennick tapped Michael on the shoulder. "In five minutes there'll be cops all over the place. Let's get out of here!"

120

Michael nodded. He put his pistol away and told Alfred to do the same. While Josey took her jacket and small traveling case from the closet, Rennick put his coat on and went over to the body of the man Emil had left behind. He took the .38 Special out of the unresisting fingers.

He put the gun in his pocket and looked at Michael and Alfred. "Any objections?"

The brothers shook their heads. Alfred took Chili by the arm and, followed by Michael, hustled her out to the gray Cadillac. In a moment, Rennick and Josey joined them. Alfred slammed the big car into reverse, turned it around and zoomed down the driveway to the coast highway.

"Easy does it," warned Rennick. "We're just some sightseers on an afternoon drive."

But the speedometer needle crept up to fifty and began to reach sixty.

"Slow down, you damn fool!" Rennick reached over the front seat and thumped a fist into Alfred's back.

"I'm not taking orders from you!" whined Alfred, looking for support from Michael.

Michael slapped him lightly on the shoulder. "He's right. Take it easy!"

Alfred swore but eased up on the throttle. In a few minutes they approached the center of the city and were slowed by red lights and auto and truck traffic.

"Damn it," said Michael, "at this rate we'll never get out of town!"

"We're not leaving town," said Rennick quietly.

Michael turned and looked back at Rennick, his small dark face suddenly unpleasant. "Take another look at your britches, buddy. They're not as big as you think!"

"This car's already hot!" said Rennick. "That motel owner back there can describe it right down to the number of threads on every stud. We get out on the highway and we're dead. We've got to get rid of this crate, the sooner the better, and get another one."

"We'll steal one!" put in Alfred.

"We'll buy one," corrected Rennick.

Michael looked back at Rennick again, but this time there was respect in his glance. "You're right," he admitted.

121

"What about the Studebaker we left at the restaurant?" said Josey.

"Too risky," said Rennick. "Emil's no fool. He'll turn that license number over to the cops first chance he gets. We've got to get rid of this one by leaving it in a storage garage. We tell them we want to leave it a week. Then we send you girls out to buy us another one—you won't be as noticeable as the rest of us."

Michael nodded. "We'll have to work fast—and what about the slot?"

"Leave it in the car," said Rennick.

"We've got to keep it with us."

"For god's sakes why?"

"It's important, that's why," said Michael.

"Why's it important?" Rennick demanded.

Michael looked away. "All I know is we've got to hang onto it."

"You're lying," said Rennick. He glanced at the machine which was on the floor beside his feet. "But I'll play ball. Put the damn thing in a box and leave it where it is. Tie it with string. The girls can go back to the garage later with the new car and pick it up."

"Yeah," nodded Michael.

Alfred parked for a few minutes in front of a liquor store while Michael went in and got a large cardboard carton. The slot machine was placed inside and the flaps were tied down. They drove on a few more blocks and parked again. Rennick gave Josey back her two thousand dollars and told her to buy a used car a couple of years old. Rennick and the two brothers got out. Arrangements were made to pick Michael and Alfred up later at a drug store nearby. Rennick was to wait at another drug store a block further back.

The Cadillac drove on and the three men split up. Strolling unhurriedly along the crowded sidewalk, Rennick went to the drug store and thumbed through magazine after magazine at the colorful stand near the front windows. After a while he bought a couple of magazines and sat in a booth. He ordered a sandwich and a pineapple malt, remaining in the booth reading the magazines long after he'd finished the food. He was not surprised when an hour and then two hours passed—there was plenty of red tape in buying a car. He

122

couldn't expect Josey to close the deal too fast—that would only make her look suspicious.

He bought more magazines and was well started on them when Chili came into the store. After he paid his check at the cashier's counter, Chili stopped him near the door.

She held Rennick's arm tightly. "I'm scared," she said.

"That's nothing new," said Rennick. "We're all scared."

"Its different with me." Chili brushed her fingers nervously through her short dark curls. "Josey's got you but I've got nobody I can trust. I don't like those other two."

"They were pretty good when it got rough back there," Rennick reminded her.

"I know, but—" She glanced toward the street. "Can I trust you, I mean really trust you?"

"Sure."

"Well—" Chili hesitated.

"We haven't got much time," said Rennick.

"I better not." Chili turned abruptly and left the store.

Rennick followed her out to the street where a cream-colored Pontiac sedan was double-parked. Josey was at the wheel and the two brothers were sitting beside her in the front seat. Rennick and Chili got in back.

"Cream's a hell of a noticeable color," said Rennick, as they got under way.

"It was the only thing they could sell us in a hurry," explained Josey. "I'm sorry."

"It'll be okay," said Rennick. "Stop at the first hotel you see and let the others out."

Alfred twisted around in the front seat. "Who's giving who the bum's rush?"

"Shut up, loud mouth," said Rennick. "We split. They'll be watching for five people like us. Josey and me will stay at another motel and you three stay somewhere else till the heat's off."

"Who keeps the car?" demanded Michael.

"Josey paid for it," shrugged Rennick. "We keep it."

"I smell the old double X," said Michael. "Alfred and me keep the car or it's no dice."

"And what's to keep you two from running out?"

"You're going to trust us because we trust you," said

123

Michael. "And there's still the boat deal, don't forget. I owe that Emil bastard plenty for what he did to Rosemary."

"We're not forgetting," said Rennick.

When they reached the city's outskirts, Josey parked the car for a few minutes. Rennick took over the wheel while Michael and Alfred joined Chili in the back. The three in back got down on the floor, remaining there while Rennick drove a mile to a small but well-kept motel that had front and rear entrances. Rennick went inside and registered. Returning to the sedan, he drove it to the unit he'd rented, No. 9, and parked it in the open-air garage next door. He and Josey went inside. In about five minutes, the cream-colored sedan went past the window, Alfred driving, Michael and Chili not in view because they were still down on the floor. As prearranged, Alfred drove out the rear way to prevent the motel owner, in his front office, from noticing that the car had left.

Josey put her arms around Rennick's neck and kissed him tenderly on the cheek and then on the mouth. "Alone again," she smiled. "And, thanks to you, darling, we're safe —for a while at least. You were wonderful the way you took over, but—" She frowned slightly. "Why did you let them have the car?"

"That leaves them thinking we're playing ball," said Rennick. He felt good. He put his arms around her slim waist, lifted her till her face was level with his and rubbed his nose against hers. "As soon as it gets dark we're shoving off. Riding a bus'll be risky but at least we'll be on our own again."

"Yes," said Josey slowly.

When he set her down, she walked over to the dresser and opened her traveling case. She took out a clear plastic comb, removed the gold barrettes and started to run the comb through her yellow hair with short, deft—almost angry—strokes.

"Does that mean that we're skipping the boat?" she asked after a while.

"My god," said Rennick, "you're not still thinking about that—not after what happened to Rosemary!"

Josey turned away from the mirror. Her large gray eyes were cool and direct. "I am."

"Are you crazy? Have you forgotten already what happened to Laurette and Vodka? What's the matter with you?"

"Nothing's the matter with me."

"Then you must be plain dumb!" Rennick put his hands on her shoulders and gripped them so tightly he knew he must be hurting her. "Have you ever heard about the law of averages and how it gets its hooks into a guy? Well, you've been wanting to know what's wrong with me and I'll tell you what's wrong with me—and maybe it'll knock some sense into you!"

Josey tried to interrupt him, but he rushed on, getting angrier by the moment. "I had a friend, see, a guy by the name of Bob May. We went through boot camp together, we got sent to Pendleton together, we even went overseas in the same outfit. We drank from the same canteen, wore the same shirt—he was a brother to me and he meant more to me than my own brother who was nothing but a lousy draft dodger. I don't know where the hell he is now and I don't care—my brother, I mean. The same with my mother—she was a rotten tramp who was drunk all the time and I don't know where she is and I don't care, understand?"

Still holding Josey's shoulders, he glared down at her. "And I'm not telling you this to make you soft-hearted, understand? I'm telling you about the law of averages. May and me went through every battle our outfit was in—guys in our platoon got killed and wounded, but May and me kept right on going, never got scratched. We even put in for the worst job of all—frogmen—because we figured nothing could hit us, nothing could happen to us. But the law of averages was laughing at us all the time . . ."

Rennick turned away and walked over to the window. He remembered it all too plainly, the dark water in the pre-dawn hours, the pitching of the rubber rafts as they paddled away from the wet flanks of the submarine.

The anger went out of his voice. "It was cold that morning and we all had a shot of whiskey before we got into the rafts. I was a wise guy and took along the bottle and I kept taking a nip now and then as we paddled in. When we dove in and swam under water to look for barricades, I was feeling no pain. We didn't see any barricades—I didn't, anyway. I was too drunk to see anything. We swam all the way to shore, me and May and about seven others, and made a

125

quick reconnaissance and it was about then that the Japs spotted us—a whole god damn platoon of 'em. I don't know what all happened but they tell me I was hell on wheels. I remember shooting four or five and strangling one. But I don't remember none of that the way I remember killing May. I was so god damn drunk I didn't know what I was doing and when May ran in front of me I thought he was a Jap and I shot him. I shot him right in the head, right behind the ear. The guy who was a brother to me, the guy who got himself court-martialed for stealing quinine for me when I had malaria . . ."

Rennick stood before the window, looking out at the driveway without really seeing it.

Josey came over and took his hand. "Darling," she said, softy, "I'm—"

"They gave me a medal for it!" said Rennick angrily. "I was a big god damn hero for shooting my best friend! The President put that damn blue ribbon around my neck and every god damn paper in the country ran the picture. Officers saluted me—but it didn't last long. Six months later they bounced me out of the Corps. I'd been drunk on duty about six times!"

Josey tried to speak but he went on angrily. "See what I mean about the law of averages? It's hanging around there all the time and eventually it gets you. It got May. It got Laurette and Vodka. It got Rosemary. It's been getting closer and closer, Josey, and the next time it'll be you. It was nearly you this afternoon, but it turned out to be Rosemary instead. Now the hooks are waiting for you, really waiting for you."

Rennick turned suddenly and caught her up in his arms. He held her tightly, feeling the roundness of her breasts where they pressed his chest. "That's why the boat deal's out, Josey, I'd go crazy if something happened to you. I'd kill myself if something happened to you. A person gets so many narrow escapes—you had the big one this afternoon— and the next one will be for keeps!"

He kissed her mouth fiercely, moving his lips against hers to taste the full sweetness of them.

"It's not for myself that I'm afraid," he said. "I'm too god damn tough to die. It's you that's got me scared!"

"I know, darling," she said gently. "And I love you for it. I love you very much."

Josey unclasped her hands from around his neck and ran her fingers slowly down his back. The thrill of her touch went deep into him, tantalizing him, arousing him.

"You shouldn't blame yourself for what happened to your friend," she said. "You didn't know what you were doing. And they wouldn't have given you the medal if you hadn't deserved it."

He brushed his lips against the corner of her mouth. "You're good for me, Josey. I don't think about May very much when I'm with you. And I don't feel so guilty about what happened. Sometimes, though, I can't help it. Because —drunk or sober—it was me that pulled the trigger."

Josey nodded. "I guess I know what you mean. I guess we all have things we can't help. Like the way I feel about you." Lightly she ran her fingers across the muscle of his shoulder. "I want you. I always want you—it's something I can't help."

He bent his head and kissed the small shadow between her breasts in the deep V of her yellow blouse. "That's something I don't want you to help."

"But there are other things," said Josey. "One other thing especially."

She looked away, her large gray eyes distant and discontent.

"When I was a little girl," she said, "my family was just average. Our car was always a few years old, we rented our house and my mother was always trying to save a dime here and a nickel there. Then when I was twelve, my father got a wonderful promotion to manager of a branch insurance office in San Diego, a big branch. We bought a big house and my mother had a maid and I got lots of new dresses— and one of them was just darling, and organdy with red beads in front. I loved that dress and I loved the little electric stove my father bought me and the real china dishes and the bicycle and my very own room with my own dresser with mirrors and my own bed and my own closet. And I had a fountain pen to take to school and new shoes whenever my old ones got the slightest little bit scuffed. And, best of all,

127

on my birthday my father gave me a gold wrist watch set with two little diamonds . . ."

A small smile of resignation passed over her mouth. "It all lasted not quite a year before my father died. A hemorrhage. My mother had to sell the house and go to work. She sold everything. My toys, the bicycle and the little stove, even my best dresses, even the organdy with the red beads. And the wrist watch—they gave her sixteen dollars and seventy-five cents for my wonderful wrist watch . . ."

"Must've been tough," said Rennick. "But you were just a kid, you probably got—"

"No, I never got over it. If we'd never been rich, I wouldn't have minded. But to have all those things, to be rich for one year and then poor for years afterward—it was terrible!"

Josey shuddered and clung to Rennick. "I know I sound foolish, but it's something I can't help. That's why I quit teaching school and joined up with Emil. That's why I want to go through with the boat deal . . ."

"My god," said Rennick, "what's it worth if you get your head shot off?"

"But I won't," she said. "Nothing can happen to me as long as you're along, John. I know it. I can just feel it."

"I don't believe in hunches any more," he said. "The deal's off."

"You won't change your mind?"

"Not a chance. The dough isn't that important to me. But you are."

"Can't I make you change your mind, John?"

He shook his head. "Not a chance."

"I don't give up easily, darling." She walked slowly across the room and pulled the cord that shut the venetian blind. Turning around, she unbuttoned her blouse, slipped out of it and dropped it slowly onto the bed. She unfastened the hooks at the side of her skirt, unzippered it and let it slide down her legs. Bending forward, she reached behind her back and unhooked her bra. She dropped it slowly, deliberately, onto the bed. Her fingers traced across the embroidery at the side of her green panties.

"We're back to Friday," she said softly.

128

Rennick did not reply. He stood stiffly over by the dresser, trying not to watch her.

"This may be the last time," she said, "because if you don't go I'll go anyway, with Alfred and Michael . . ."

"You're a fool!" said Rennick.

She rolled the green panties down over the curve of her hip and stepped out of them. She was naked then except for the black high-heeled pumps which accented the long slimness of her legs. Stretching idly, she raised her arms over her head and went up on tip-toe. She filled her lungs with air and he couldn't help admiring the way the room's shadows emphasized the hollow where her belly was sucked in. She expelled her breath slowly and walked over to him. She stopped, looked up into his eyes, and then moved closer until the tips of her breasts were touching his shirt. She swayed back and forth slightly, letting her breasts brush against him.

Rennick stood there stiffly, his hands turning into fists at his sides.

"I don't blame you for not wanting to go," she said.

She took his hand, raised it up and opened the fingers. She placed it over her right breast, pressing it with her own warm hand.

"Damn you!" said Rennick. He squeezed the firm flesh hard.

She reached up and unbuttoned his shirt. Her gray eyes were dancing. She drew her fingernails slowly down across his chest, scratching him not deeply but enough to leave white marks in the skin.

"Damn you!" she said. "Damn you, damn you!"

He threw his arms around her. His hands swept up and down her back, his fingers digging angrily into her flesh.

"I love you, John," she whispered. "I love you so very, very much!"

She sighed with delight when he picked her up and threw her roughly on the bed.

"God damn you!" he said, unbuttoning his shirt the rest of the way.

13

BEHIND THEM, THE CALIFORNIA COAST WAS MANY MILES distant, its coves and rolling hills and beaches blended together in gray and green lines that lay flat and low against the horizon. It was a clear, clean afternoon with bright sunshine. The ocean was a deep restless blue. Rennick stood behind the polished mahogany wheel and kept the trim white Chris-Craft headed slightly northwest. The waves were only moderately high and the boat sliced through them at a steady 15 knots. He was glad that they had been able to rent a 30-footer—anything smaller would've been uncomfortable this far out.

"Still no sign of them," said Josey impatiently. She turned slowly, studying the water ahead through a pair of large binoculars. "You sure we're going the right way?"

Rennick shrugged. He placed his finger against the cabin's blue-tinted windshield and pointed at a sharp nose of land that jutted out on the west side of the big island which lay just ahead.

"That's West Point," he said. "Anyway that's what the chart says. I figure Emil's anchored around on the other side."

"Maybe he changed plans," said Josey, raising the glasses to her eyes again.

"I hope he did," said Rennick. "I hope we never see the son of a bitch."

"Now, John. You know everything's going to be all right."

"I wish I was as sure as you are. And I wish to hell we knew what's supposed to be on the boat. You still think Michael doesn't know?"

She nodded. "He doesn't know. He'd have told me if he did."

"That's a laugh," Rennick said bitterly.

"Don't be so glum, darling." She stepped over to him, kissed him lightly on the cheek and opened the door. "Maybe I can see better from up front."

She closed the door and through the window he watched her go forward and join Michael and Alfred. She was very trim in her brown slacks and pink sweater. Picking up one of the rifles the two men were cleaning, she sighted experimentally along its barrel and then set it down. She raised the binoculars to her eyes again and scanned the horizon.

The door opened behind Rennick and Chili came into the cabin. She said nothing. Leaning against the bulkhead, she lit a cigarette with a small silver lighter. She watched Rennick for a moment through the smoke, then turned and watched the others up forward.

"You never did tell me why you were locked in that closet," said Rennick after a while.

"No, I didn't," said Chili.

She continued to look out through the windshield. As they approached the more open water near the point, the boat began to pitch a little more noticeably. Chili turned away from the windshield and clutched his arm. Her face was so pale he thought she might be sick.

"John," she said suddenly, "turn the boat around."

He looked at her in surprise.

"It's not going to work," she said, shaking his arm.

"What's got into you?" he demanded.

"Nothing."

"Then why all the sudden dramatics"

"I just know it's not going to work." Her brown eyes pleaded with him. "Please turn back!"

"And look even more yellow than I've looked up to now?" Rennick shook his head. "We've gone this far—there's no backing out now."

"But it's so foolish!"

He looked at her sharply. "Is there something you know that the rest of us don't know?"

"No."

"Then forget it—and keep your head down when the shooting starts."

"But I tell you—"

Chili's voice broke off as a shout came from Josey up near the prow. Lowering the binoculars, Josey ran back along the railing and entered the cabin.

"I've seen them!" she said. Handing the glasses to Ren-

131

nick, she pointed to the northwest. "They're a long way off."

Rennick turned the wheel over to Josey and raised the glasses to his eyes. He expected the find the *Golden Cloud* in the channel between the two islands but instead it was far to the northwest of Santa Rosa. He judged it to be a good ten or twelve miles off the island. It was so far away that occasionally a large swell hid it from view, except for the tall masts. He noticed that a small boat, a cruiser smiliar to the Chris-Craft, was drawn alongside.

"What do you figure the small boat's for?" He handed Josey back the binoculars and took over the wheel.

"That's the boat he's rendezvousing with."

She looked through the glasses again. After a while she said carefully: "What did Chili want?"

Rennick glanced around the cabin. He hadn't noticed that Chili had left.

"Nothing," he lied.

"She's in love with you," said Josey. "Did you know that?"

He laughed and put his arm around her shoulder. "Where'd you dream that up?"

"She's crazy about you." Josey's large gray eyes looked up at him seriously. "It's written all over her. Damn her, she just doesn't respect other people's property!"

"How much am I worth to the acre?" he said.

"It's not funny, darling." Josey squeezed his arm lightly and walked to the door. "I'll give her a talking to she won't forget!"

"Go easy on her," said Rennick. "She's scared to death."

As Josey went out, Michael came in carrying an M-1 rifle and several clips of ammunition for it. He laid the rifle on the cardboard carton which contained the slot machine.

"How about your revolver?" he asked. "Got enough slugs for it?"

Rennick nodded. He cut the boat's speed and began a broad circle off to the left.

"What's the pitch?" said Michael. He took off his glasses and wiped drops of spray from them. His small dark eyes were suspicious.

"You want them to spot us?" said Rennick. "We'll cruise around here until it gets dark. Then we hit 'em."

Michael considered the matter carefully for a moment

132

before agreeing. Then he went out to inform Alfred. During the remainder of the afternoon, Rennick kept the Chris-Craft circling at half-speed in the channel between the two islands. From time to time, he watched the *Golden Cloud* through the binoculars. The small boat remained tied up at the yacht's port side. When it grew dusk, Rennick gave the Chris-Craft full throttle. A stiff cold breeze had blown up and as he headed out of the channel toward open sea again, the boat pitched sharply and spray splashed the windshield. In an hour, it was dark. It was too early for the moon to rise, bu the *Golden Cloud* was well-lighted and he had no difficulty keeping his bearings. He laid down strict rules that no lights or cigarettes were to show on the Chris-Craft.

When they were a mile from the yacht, he again cut to half-speed. He began a broad slow circle that would bring them to the leeward side of the *Golden Cloud* on their final approach. He hoped the wind would keep the men on the yacht from hearing the Chris-Craft's engine until they were within a few hundred yards.

The cabin door opened and Josey and Chili came in. They stood silently beside Rennick in the darkness as the minutes dragged by.

"It's this waiting that gets me," said Josey.

"Me too," Chili shivered and rubbed her hands together. "I could sure use a drink."

"Forget it," said Rennick. He watched the lights on the larger ship loom closer. He could make out the portholes and the folding stairway that led down the port side almost to the surface of the water. The small cruiser that had been tied up there in the afternoon apparently had finished its business. It was nowhere in sight. He let his gaze travel slowly over the yacht from the long sleek bow to the stern. No men were in view anywhere.

When there were only a hundred more yards to go, he reduced the speed to three knots and turned the wheel over to Josey. He picked up the rifle and dropped the clips of heavy 30-30 ammunition into his pocket.

"Take her in to the gangway," he told Josey, "and when you see me drop my arm put her in reverse."

He opened the bolt on the rifle and made sure there was

133

a cartridge in the chamber. "And then, god damn it, you two get down on the floor and stay there!"

He went forward and joined Michael and Alfred who knelt behind packing cases stacked near the bow. Both brothers held rifles. He put his rifle down on the deck, picked up the roll of stiff line and ducked a blast of stinging spray that the wind whipped over the prow. Then he knelt behind the packing cases and waited. He suddenly felt good. He welcomed back as old friends the feeling of tenseness and the keen pounding of his arteries.

Not until they were a few yards from the gangway did anyone appear above decks on the yacht. A man in dungarees came to the railing, looked over and turned quickly away.

Rennick stood up, holding the coil of line in his right hand and the end in his left. He signaled to Josey and she put the engine in reverse. The Chris-Craft rushed in near the stairway and then slowed perceptibly as the propeller's blades took hold. White water surged through the quickly narrowing gap between the two vessels, and the man in dungarees reappeared near the railing, a pistol in his hand.

As Rennick tossed the line upward, Alfred's rifle cracked. Rennick watched the loop of hemp settle around the chrome cleat and from the corner of his eye saw the man at the railing fall forward. He snugged the line tight, dropped to his knee, looped the end around the cleat on the Chris-Craft and secured it. When he glanced up again, the man was hanging face down over the railing and the pistol was just beginning to fall from his limp fingers.

Rennick grabbed up his rifle and signaled to Josey to keep the motor idling. He ran to the prow and leaped over open water to the gangway. He took the steps two at a time, feeling the gangway quiver below him as Michael and Alfred followed. They got to the top of the stairs, ran along the deck for a few steps and crouched together behind a white, tarp-covered lifeboat which hung from davits.

"We stick together!" Rennick told the brothers. "And don't kill Georgetti unless you have to. I got things to ask that boy!"

A full minute ticked off.

Then there was a blaze of gunfire from the base of the

thick foremast and the lifeboat shook and shuddered. Splinters flew against Rennick's neck.

"Son of a bitch!" he said. "A machine-gun!"

He sent two quick shots in the direction of the muzzle-blast and Michael did the same but the machine-gun continued to fire. Its slugs were high and wide but it would be only a moment until that was corrected. Turning, Rennick slapped Michael on the shoulder and ran in a crouch back toward the stern. Followed by Alfred, they went around the stern and along the starboard side until they were fairly amidships. The machine-gun was quiet now. A light on the foremast illuminated a man who crouched near its base. Some sixth sense caused him to turn his head. Seeing them, he swung the machine-gun around but before he could hit the trigger Rennick and Michael lifted their rifles and cut him down. The machine-gun, an old Thompson .45, hit the deck, skidded a few feet and was snatched up by another pair of hands that appeared from the other side of the foremast. At the same time, a man they hadn't noticed before— a man who looked like Sutro—opened up on them from the wheelhouse. But before he could find the range, someone else threw the yacht's master switch and all the lights went out. Rennick, Michael and Alfred flattened out on the deck as bullets hammered into a metal ventilator above them and went singing out to sea. Bits of hot lead dropped onto the back of Rennick's hand, burning the flesh slightly and giving off the odor of singed hair. He rolled over and crawled back toward the stern, followed by Michael and Alfred.

The shooting stopped. Except for the hum of the wind in the rigging and a door that gusts kept slamming somewhere, the ship was silent. Rennick's eyes strained through the darkness as he tried to determine whether Emil's men were changing their positions. He knew approximately where Sutro and the man with the Thompson were, but the whereabouts of the rest of the crew was still a mystery.

"See anything?" whispered Alfred hoarsely, his face a thin silhouette.

Rennick shook his head. Another minute passed and then he heard a scraping noise behind them. He looked around just in time to see a trapdoor open in the deck less than ten feet away. Two men popped up in the opening, the door

135

resting on their shoulders. One of them had the machine-gun and it began to spray wildly. From then on everything Rennick did was instinctive. He got his rifle turned around but there wasn't time to aim it. Firing it from the hip like a pistol, he snapped a pair of shots at the men, saw one hit its mark and the other miss. He heard Michael's M-1 cut loose at his side and wondered what was wrong with Alfred until he saw the little man fall forward, his arms twitching. Rennick emptied his rifle at the men under the door. The heavy slugs hit a hinge, the door bucked like a surfboard and one of the men flopped down the hole out of view. A moment later, the man with the machine-gun screamed and went down, the trapdoor slamming across the machine-gun. About six inches of the barrel stuck out from under the door, wedged against the edge of the deck. Rennick ran over and seized the barrel, ignoring the pain inflicted by the hot steel, and lifted the door open. The man who'd been firing the gun was huddled on wooden steps leading below decks, his chin resting on his chest, one hand still clutching the stock of the machine gun. When Rennick pulled the gun away, the man slipped off his perch and rolled and bounced to the bottom of the stairway, landing on top of his companion. Both men became sprawled shadows that did not move. Rennick watched them a moment and then eased the trapdoor shut. Carrying the Thompson, he returned to Michael and Alfred.

Michael was kneeling over the body of his brother. "The bastards!" he said softly. "The dirty bastards!"

Rennick dropped down beside him. He saw at a glance that nothing could be done for Alfred. A slug had gone in through the knobby cheekbone and ranged up through the brain.

Rennick squeezed Michael's shoulder gently. "At least it was quick . . ." He paused. "Come on. Can't be many left."

Silently Michael got to his feet and followed Rennick along the starboard railing. Rennick noticed movement on top of the wheelhouse and was tempted to snap a few shots in its direction but decided to wait for a better target. He took a few more steps and then he saw the man on the rooftop raise up on his elbows and sight a rifle. He was close enough now so he could definitely see who the man was. Sutro. There was a bandage around his left arm. Rennick

136

ducked back behind a pile of tarp-covered cases and signaled for Michael to do the same.

"Yellow bastards!" shouted Sutro. "C'mon out and fight!"

He sent several shots crashing into the pile of cases and Rennick heard the tinkle of breaking glass. Peering around the edge of a box, Rennick saw that Sutro was playing it smart. Because of the flatness of the wheelhouse roof, only Sutro's rifle and part of one hand were visible. From his vantage point, he controlled a major portion of the deck and the only way he could be successfully combated would be from an equal height. Rennick looked up into the rigging but the first glance told him that wouldn't work. Sutro would have him sighted in before he could climb more than a few feet and he'd be exposed all the way. Another bullet smacked into the cases and he drew his head back.

"What're you going to do?" said Michael. His thin face glistened with sweat.

"I'm going to get him," said Rennick. He worked his way to the other side of the pile and studied a lifeboat which hung from davits about twenty feet away. It wasn't quite high enough but it would have to do.

He darted suddenly from the protection of the wooden cases across the open deck, hearing Sutro's rifle crack as he ran. Splinters kicked up on the deck beside him and then he was behind the shelter of the lifeboat. He tossed the Thompson up onto the tarpaulin that covered the boat. Then he jumped up and caught the gunwale. His weight made the boat sway in its davits and he knew that would tip off Sutro but there was nothing he could do about it now. Throwing his legs upward, he hooked a foot over the gunwale and pulled himself up.

He scrambled across the taut surface of the tarp and found the Thompson, but before he could aim it the tarp ripped in two directions at once, dropping him inside the boat just as Sutro's rifle cracked again. The bullets went close overhead, so close they would've drilled him if the tarp hadn't torn. Slowly he raised his head until he could see Sutro lying on the roof. He sighted the Thompson in and squeezed the trigger gently, getting off half a dozen slugs. He swore as they shot harmlessly over Sutro's head—it had been a long time since he'd fired a Thompson and he'd forgotten that a machine-gun kicked upward. He aimed at the wheelhouse a foot below Sutro's head and fired a long burst.

Sutro rolled over. He yelled and dropped his rifle. He picked it up, started to aim at Rennick, changed his mind and stood up. Turning, he ran two steps along the edge of the roof before Rennick's next burst caught him. He dropped his rifle again and grabbed his middle. For a long moment he teetered on one foot at the edge of the roof and then screaming hoarsely he went over. His body glanced off the railing, droppd swiftly and kicked up a high splash when it struck the water.

Rennick jumped down from the lifeboat and returned to the pile of cases where Michael still crouched. They did not speak. Each took up a station at a corner of the pile and watched for movement in the shadowed portions of the ship. They waited for a long time. Five minutes. Ten minutes. Nothing moved. All was silent except for the cold wind in the rigging and the slap of the waves against the ship's flanks.

"How many you figure are left?" Rennick asked.

Michael held up one finger. "Just Emil."

"Let's get him." Rennick removed the Thompson's ammunition drum, saw that it was still half loaded and replaced it. He got the .38 Special out of his pocket, broke it open and checked the chambers. All were loaded.

They left the pile of cases and went silently along the deck, Michael trailing about five paces behind. They made a complete, careful circle around the deck without seeing anyone. Then Rennick opened the highly polished mahogany door to the companionway that led below decks. Going down through the gloom a step at a time, they reached a short passageway in which burned two dim emergency bulbs that apparently were not connected with the yacht's main light system. Along the right wall were the doors to a few staterooms and up ahead was a door Rennick recognized. It led to the wardroom where he'd met Vodka. One by one he tested the stateroom doors—all were locked. He went to the end of the passageway and tested the wardroom's brass knob. It was unlocked.

"Guard the door," he told Michael.

He went in. An emergency light glowed near one of the open portholes, reflecting dimly on the shiny waxed surfaces

138

of the tables. On a divan at the far end of the wardroom reclined what looked like the figure of a man. Rennick approached cautiously until he saw that the figure was only a twisted olive drab blanket. Hearing a scuffling sound back at the doorway, he raised the Thompson and started to turn around.

"Freeze, you crumb!"

The voice came from behind him. It was Emil's voice, deadly and ugly.

"Drop the gun on the blanket!"

Rennick hesitated. A dozen thoughts crowded his brain at once. He wondered what had happened to Michael and what chance he'd have if he tried to spin around and cut Emil down.

"One more second!" Emil's words were high-pitched, anxious.

Rennick dropped the Thompson onto the divan. Then he stood there, waiting, hands held stiff at his sides.

"Turn around," said Emil. "Slow!"

Rennick turned until he was facing Emil. Barefoot, Emil stood in the doorway, gripping another Thompson. A gold-braided yachting cap was pushed to the back of his head and he wore blue denim slacks and a white T-shirt which his muscular shoulders filled well. His plump face was pale and drawn and there was a crafty expression in his eyes.

"Where's your virility now?" Emil demanded abruptly.

Rennick said nothing. He watched Emil gesture fiercely with the machine-gun.

"Why don't you show off your manly figure now?" demanded Emil.

Rennick remained silent.

"You had Josey, didn't you?" Emil's plump lips twisted. "How many times did you have her?"

He shook the gun at Rennick. "Answer me! How many times?"

"It's none of your god damn business!"

"Then you admit it!" Emil's voice rose to almost a scream. "You bastard. You thieving bastard! And you had Vodka too. My Vodka! Answer me! Didn't you have Vodka!"

Rennick kept his eyes on the Thompson. Knuckles white,

139

Emil clutched the stock tightly, his finger playing with the trigger.

"And what about Laurette?" he demanded shrilly. "You wanted her. Don't try to lie to me! I can see it in your eyes. You wanted my darling Laurette just like Rudolpho."

"You're crazy!" said Rennick.

The room was silent for a moment. Emil expelled his breath slowly.

When he spoke again, his voice was subdued, almost normal. "There's nothing wrong with me."

Again he filled his lungs with air, his broad chest swelling against the thin cotton of the white T-shirt and quite suddenly Rennick was reminded of the oil painting which hung in Georgetti's house. The painting had shown a muscular man lifting a bar bell. Now he knew it was supposed to be Emil. It was a fairly good representation except that Emil's belly was fat and soft, while the painting had shown it to be flat and slim.

"I'm going to kill Josey," said Emil, almost matter-of-factly. "I'm not going to kill her because she wanted my yacht and came out here to get it. I'm going to kill her because she gave herself to you. I'm going to stand her up in front of you, Rennick, and I'm going to riddle her with bullets. I'm going to shoot her face off and I'm going to shoot her breasts and I'm going to shoot her nice long legs and then I'm going to dump the whole bloody mess of her on top of you, Rennick, and then I'm going to kill you!"

Rennick raised his fists. "You god damn crazy fool!"

He started toward Emil. He wasn't sure what he could do against the Thompson but he knew he had to make the attempt. He took one step and then Michael appeared on his knees in the doorway, an M-1 at his shoulder. Michael weaved back and forth drunkenly and began to fire.

14

MICHAEL'S FIRST BULLET HIT EMIL IN THE SHOULDER AND spun him halfway around. His second bullet hit Emil in the thigh and spun him the rest of the way around. Emil screamed with pain and dropped the Thompson without firing a shot. As a dot of red appeared on the shoulder of his white T-shirt, he turned around again, stiff-leggedly trying to keep his balance. When he hit the floor, the dot at his shoulder had grown to the size of a bright, scarlet saucer. He lay there silently, his legs tangled grotesquely, his body quiet except for the trigger finger of his right hand which jerked convulsively in a frustrated effort to reach the Thompson which lay a few inches away.

Picking up the gun, Rennick went to the doorway. He helped Michael to his feet.

"Damn it," he said, "I'd of liked to have you in my platoon, Mike, glasses and all!"

"He come up behind me." Tenderly Michael touched a deep gash over his right ear. "Clobbered me with something. I'd of got back sooner but I had to crawl down the hall where he threw the rifle . . ." He looked at the blood smeared on his fingertips. "Damn it, it's sure red!"

"You'll be okay," said Rennick, "but I don't know about Emil."

He bent over the fallen man and felt his pockets to make sure he was unarmed. He saw that the shoulder wound, though bloody, was not too serious. The thigh wound, however, looked like another matter. The high-powered rifle bullet had gone into the pelvis.

"I'd just as soon let the son of a bitch die . . ." Rennick shrugged at Michael, "but we can't let him just lay there. Help me get him up."

Michael took Emil's shoulders and Rennick his legs and they lifted him onto the divan. Eyes closed, Emil breathed irregularly as the red stain in his denim slacks grew darker and larger. Rennick unfastened Emil's belt, opened the zipper and tried to pull the slacks down but the stickiness of the blood glued the cloth to Emil's skin.

He heard someone running down the companionway steps and looked up as Josey came through the doorway.

"John, are you all right?" Fear shadowed her large gray eyes as she looked first at Rennick and then at Emil's silent form. She ran to Rennick and threw her arms around him. She clung to him tightly. Her cheek was cold from the wind outside but her tears were warm.

"My darling, my darling!" she whispered.

Her fingers twisted in the lapels of his jacket as she turned her face up to him. Her eyes were red-rimmed and her lipstick was worn to a pale pink.

"I died a dozen times, John. All that shooting and then the silences—the silences were the worst. I was sure you were dead. I was positive and I knew that if it hadn't been for me you wouldn't have done it. And I thought about what you said about the law of averages and I got sick, sick to my stomach . . ."

"It's over," said Rennick. He placed his hands gently on her cheeks and kissed her, noticing as he did so that his fingers were red with Emil's blood.

Dropping his hands to his sides, he wiped his fingers on his trousers but the blood was already dried and would not rub off.

"We've won," said Josey. She gave him another hug, her eyes suddenly sparkling. "I can hardly believe it—but we won!"

She went over to Emil and searched through his pockets until she found a ring of keys. Lifting them high, she shook them triumphantly. Then she took Rennick's hand and led him to the doorway.

"Come," she said, "I want to show you something."

As he passed through the door, Rennick looked back at Emil who still lay unmoving on the divan.

"Keep your eye on him," he told Michael.

Michael nodded.

Josey went out into the companionway and unlocked one of the stateroom doors. Pushing it open, she went in and Rennick followed. The stateroom was dark but there was enough light to see that it was stacked from ceiling to roof with wooden cases.

"Scotch," said Josey. "From Canada. The most expensive Scotch money can buy."

"Whiskey!" Rennick laughed bitterly. "Just what I need!"

Opening the doors to the other staterooms, Josey revealed that they were stacked high with more wooden cases.

"There's more piled on the deck," she added, "and probably the rest is in the hold. Emil bought it all for a song."

She took Rennick's hand again and started toward the steps, "And there's something else."

"Wait a minute," said Rennick. He held her hand tightly, forcing her to halt.

He looked down at her and he could feel the muscle knotting along his jaw.

"You lied to me, Josey. You said you didn't know what was on the boat."

She twisted her fingers, trying to free herself. "You're hurting me, John," she said softly.

"You lied to me, didn't you?"

She looked up at him, her eyes meeting his. "Yes, I lied to you."

"Why?"

"I was afraid you wouldn't go through with it if you thought I knew too much. You were already suspicious. You thought I was the girl at the piano."

"Were you?"

She shook her head. "I didn't lie to you about that darling."

"I'm not so sure now," he said.

"Please don't be so unhappy, darling." She started toward the stairway again. "This is a time for celebration. Wait till I show you the rest!"

She went up the companionway to the deck. Rennick trailed her silently. They went down the port-side gangway that led to the Chris-Craft and entered the cabin. Standing near the wheel with a cigarette in her hand, Chili stared at the ocean through the windshield.

She did not look around as they entered. "Is the blood-bath over?" she asked acidly.

"All over," said Josey.

Lifting off the cardboard carton which covered the slot machine, Josey knelt and inserted one of Emil's keys in a keyhole at the back. She opened a small hinged door and brought out a tray that was filled with quarters and two oblong pieces of a flat metal that looked like copper.

"These are the little darlings!" she said. She picked up the pieces of metal, opened her traveling case and got out a magnifying glass. She inspected them briefly. "Hardly scratched."

"What in the hell are they?" said Rennick.

"Plates," said Josey. "Counterfeit—but as good as anything the government can engrave. There's a printing press on the yacht and we'll be able to print perfect reproductions of the Federal liquor tax stamp." She looked up at him, her face glowing. "Pretty clever?"

"God damn clever," said Rennick. "Did you hide them in the slot machine?"

Josey shook her head. "No, Emil did."

"But you put the slot in the Studebaker?"

"Yes," said Josey. "One of the boys helped me."

"And then you lied to me—said you didn't know how the slot got there."

"Does it matter, darling?" Josey held the copper plates out to him. "Do you know what these mean? Not necessarily a home at Malibu, dresses by Adrian or a dozen diamond bracelets on my arm. Not necessarily a Cadillac with a gold-plated dash board . . ."

She turned the plates over and they glittered faintly in the illumination from the dome light overhead. "They mean security for two people in love, John. They mean freedom for two people in love to do anything they want to do. They mean I can sleep till noon if I want to and not rush off to a schoolroom at nine. They mean you can go down to the beach in the afternoon instead of swearing at a gang of oil men. Do you see what they mean, John?"

"Yeah, I see," he said. "And what if I'd rather swear at a bunch of grease monkeys? Then what?"

He turned and opened the cabin door.

"John, where are you going?" She tugged at his sleeve.

"To ask Emil a few questions."

As he went up the gangway he heard her behind him
144

trying to catch up. He was tempted to help her across the space between the two boats but he pushed the temptation aside. When he went down the companionway, she followed, catching up with him as he entered the wardroom. Emil was still lying on the divan. Michael stood nearby, holding his M-1 by the barrel.

Rennick bent over to Emil.

"Where's Georgetti?"

Emil did not move. Fine droplets of sweat glistened on his forehead.

"Was Georgetti one of the men we shot?" demanded Rennick.

Emil's eyes opened. They were cloudy with pain. He looked up at Rennick, glanced over at Michael and closed his eyes again.

"Faking won't do you no good now," said Rennick. "You're at the end of the line, Emil—and you know it." He began to pull the blood-stained slacks down. "I'm going to try to keep you alive—not because you're worth it but so I can get some of the answers I've been chasing for a hell of a long time."

He went out into the passageway, took down a red first-aid box that was fastened to the wall and returned to the wardroom. Opening it, he took out a packet of sulfanilamide powder and some bandages. He pulled Emil's slacks down and unbuttoned his shorts.

When he started to tug the shorts down, Emil raised a hand and weakly tried to push him away.

"No . . ." said Emil. His fingers fastened loosely onto the top of the shorts.

Rennick knocked his fingers away. "Go back to nearly the beginning. What did you mean by that crack about Rudolpho the busboy wanting Laurette? Did you kill Laurette?"

"No . . ." said Emil.

"You filthy bastard, doing the things you did to her and letting filth like Stanley and your other rats do things to her. The poor kid never had a chance. You never gave her a chance!" Rennick's voice rose. "I swore I'd get the bastard that did those things to her. I swore I'd get you, Emil!"

145

He tugged roughly at the shorts and Emil cried out as the cloth pulled away from the sticky red hole in his thigh.

But it wasn't the rifle wound that Rennick stared at. It was another injury, an old injury judging by the smooth scar tissue.

He let Emil pull the shorts part-way back up and began to sprinkle sulfanilamide on the rifle wound.

Abruptly Emil sat up. He swung a fist weakly at Rennick's head and missed.

"Now you know!" he roared. "I'm not even half a man. Does it make you feel good to be so damned superior? Is your strength bulging in your veins? Why don't you brag about your conquests and make me feel weaker? Why don't you tell me about the women you've had! Why—" His voice broke and he fell back against the divan, his fingernails tearing at the upholstery as he tried to keep from sliding to a reclining position.

"God, how I hate you, Rennick!" Emil's arm slipped down into the opening under the divan's maple armrest. "God, if I could only kill you!"

Rennick finished dusting the wound with powder. Tearing the cellophane off a bandage, he laid the thick cotton gauze over the wound and began to fasten it down with strips of adhesive.

"Say something!" screamed Emil. "Why do you all stand there looking at me like fools!" His eyes rolled drunkenly. He caught sight of Chili as she came in through the doorway. "You knew it too, didn't you? You laughed at me, like the others did, didn't you?"

Chili remained standing near the doorway. She did not reply.

Emil struggled to free his arm from where it was caught in the divan. When he spoke again, his voice was no longer a scream. It was low and hoarse.

"Anybody can see I had to kill Laurette," he said. "She gave herself to that fat slobbery Stanley. God, how he yelled when he saw the gun!"

He glanced at Rennick, his eyes becoming strangely steady. "And Vodka. She was very good. She did not scream or try to escape. But she had broken her word. She gave

146

herself to you, Rennick, so there was only one thing for me to do . . ."

Emil's eyes turned to Josey. "You whore. You hid him from me—and then you ran away with him. You bitch. You god damn wh—"

Rennick slapped Emil hard across the mouth. "Leave Josey out of this! Stick to facts. Who was the blonde at the piano—was it Laurette or Vodka?"

Emil began to laugh. "Leave her out of it! Leave the queen bee out of it? You damn fool, why don't you ask *her* who the blonde was at the piano? And why don't you ask *her* about that phone call she made when she called Michael and told him to hustle to Ventura so she could carry out her plans to take over the yacht. Ask her, you damn fool, ask—"

"Be quiet, Emil," said Josey.

"Then ask Michael," said Emil. "Ask Michael about the phone call. Didn't she phone you?"

Michael looked at Josey and then at Rennick. His hands shifted nervously along the barrel of the M-1. "Well, I don't see what difference it makes. She phoned me. She asked—"

"No, I didn't, Michael," said Josey. "I didn't phone you!"

Michael shrugged and at the same time Rennick heard a small popping sound.

Abruptly Emil began to laugh.

A faint sizzling sound, like the sizzling of a wet match, floated through the room. Rennick wondered where it was coming from and where he had heard it before. As Emil's laughter grew stronger, erupting in reverberating waves, Rennick remembered where he'd heard the sizzling sound before and recognized its danger. He strode to the divan and jammed his arm down under the arm-rest where Emil's arm had been hidden. He saw a wooden box between the divan and the wall and then he saw the grenade lying near the box and the other grenades and the cartons of pistol ammunition in the box.

He shouted a warning to the others and picked up the smoking grenade as Emil tried to push him off the divan. There was no time for thinking, no time to consider where was the best place to hurl the grenade.

He lobbed it toward the open doorway, praying that it
147

wouldn't hit the jamb or the wall and bounce back into the room.

The girls screamed and the grenade traveled slowly through the air, turning over, lazily displaying its dimpled iron sides and the rust around its timing mechanism. A small trail of bluish smoke followed it out the doorway.

Landing in the companionway, it bounced once and then exploded with a tremendous roar against the door of one of the staterooms. Pain thrust deeply into Rennick's eardrums from the concussion and the force of it slammed him up against the divan. Angry bits of the grenade whizzed past followed by a shower of splinters, jagged chunks of wood and bits of glass that flew through the doorway like small crazed birds. Pieces struck Rennick's neck and arms and he felt Michael stumble against him. He heard Josey screaming and saw her fall against Michael and through it all he heard Emil's wild laughter.

When he looked out into the companionway, it was a mass of orange and blue roaring flames. The door to the stateroom had been blown in along with half the wall and he could hear the sound of breaking glass and his nostrils tingled with the smell of smoke and burning liquor.

He saw Josey rise up from the floor, carrying Michael's rifle. A thin line of blood flowed from a cut on her cheek.

"—trying to kill us!" she screamed. She said something else, but Rennick couldn't understand her because of the crackling of the flames and the yells of the others.

She aimed the heavy rifle at the divan and it leaped in her hands once, twice, three times as she pulled the trigger, sending bullets crashing into Emil's chest and belly. Emil moved his hands weakly and rolled off the divan, landing partly on Michael who was trying to regain his feet. The rifle cracked twice more, the first bullet shattering Michael's glasses and the second entering his head through the short gray hairs at his temple. Balancing a moment on his knees, Michael turned slowly and fell across Emil.

"Jesus Christ!" roared Rennick. As he pulled the rifle away from Josey, there was a muffled explosion from one of the staterooms and long, reaching arms of blue flame curled in through the wardroom doorway. In quick succession, there were other explosions as the liquor cargo caught

148

fire. Rennick ran to the door, kicked debris out of the way and shut it with a thrust of his shoulders. Before he could back away, there was another explosion. The door buckled inward, snapped its hinges and crashed against him, knocking him to the floor. The wardroom filled with a tremendous heat that drew the very breath from his lungs. Black and greasy, an acrid smoke that stank of burned whiskey poured into the room. Coughing and gasping, his eyes running with tears, he got up again and worked his way to one of the portholes. He found the lever that opened it, bore down on it but it failed to budge. Dimly he could see that it was rusted. He went to another porthole and hit the lever with all his strength. It bent, creaked and then the glass swung open. Rennick stuck his head out, drew fresh air into his lungs and turned back to the wardroom. He found Josey and Chili cowering together near the divan. Taking Josey by the shoulders, he half-dragged and half-carried her to the porthole. Lifting her, he shoved her, legs first, through the narrow round opening. He put his lips close against her ear so she would be able to hear him above the noise of the flames.

"Can you swim?"

She nodded, but when he released her she refused to let go of the sides of the porthole.

"John!" In the crazy firelight, her face was white and tortured. "Come with me, John!"

He pried her fingers loose and pushed her through. Filling his lungs again with fresh air, he turned and went back for Chili. She did not resist when he carried her past one of the burning tables over to the porthole and pushed her through. He swung himself upward, thrust his legs through and wriggled his hips through. But his shoulders stuck in the narrow opening. Swearing, he ripped off his jacket, noticing that the fabric was smouldering in a number of small areas down the front. Again he tried to squeeze through and again he failed, realizing as he hung there that the metal ring of the porthole was growing hotter. He pulled off his shirt, extended his arms over his head and, kicking at the sides of the ship, inched his way through.

He fell half a dozen feet into the water and after the heat of the wardroom the ocean was like ice. A wave hit him and knocked him against the side of the yacht. Shivering, he

149

kicked off his slacks and shoes and swam a few strokes looking for Josey and Chili. He found them treading water aimlessly nearly amidships, far too close to the ship's side. He shouted at them but they could not understand him over the mixed sounds of the wind and the water and the flames. Gesturing at them to follow, he swam through the debris. Bits of burning wood hissed into the water near him as more explosions shook the ship. When he swam around the stern and glimpsed the Chris-Craft, he had his first feeling of panic.

The yacht's port side, where the Chris-Craft was tied, had been blown completely open, spewing flame over the small cruiser. There was a tower of fire on the Chris-Craft's cabin roof and other flames raced from the bow to the stern. He glanced up at the yacht's lifeboats which still hung in their davits on the deck. The mizzenmast had crashed down on one, cracking it like an egg, and the other was burning. Another blast occurred inside the yacht and the deck erupted all around the burning lifeboat, shattering it into a million bits. Rennick shouted at Josey and Chili and began to swim away from the boats. He saw that neither of the girls was a strong swimmer and slowed his strokes so he would stay with them.

When they were still only a hundred yards from the yacht, there was a tremendous explosion which lit the water around them as bright as day. It sounded like the fuel tanks. A broken chair shot up into the sky, flaming like a rocket and was followed by a case of whiskey which leaked fire as it came plummeting down.

Like a paper boat, the yacht folded slowly, its back broken. Its two sections formed a forty-five-degree angle as it sank hissing and steaming, regurgitating great foaming bubbles. The Chris-Craft was sucked into the vast spinning eddy and whirled like a Fourth of July pinwheel, giving off sparks and trails of smoke. When it plunged, it went swiftly, leaving behind a small whirlpool and foaming bubbles of its own.

Except for the monotonous sound of the waves and the wind, a quietness settled on the ocean. Rennick wiped the spray from his eyes and stared at the bubbles where the Chris-Craft had gone down. He thought of the twelve long miles that lay between him and the girls and safety. He felt sick to his stomach. And he was afraid.

15

RENNICK SWAM THROUGH THE DEBRIS, PAWING AT TORN boards and crushed boxes. Angrily he kicked away a length of manila line that coiled around his calves. When he saw a piece of partly submerged cloth that had the dark appearance of a life-jacket, he swam to it. He seized it and found that it was Michael's coat and Michael was still in it, his eyes protruding, as if in terror, from the force of the bullet that had passed behind them. Rennick turned away.

Twice he swam in a circle around the area of floating wreckage, hoping to find at least one life-jacket. He did not. He cursed at the size of the pieces of debris. Few of the chunks were larger than his fist. Finally, when he had given up hope, he found a four-by-four timber about six feet long to which was attached—like the cross-arm of a "T"—a strip of deck planking. It was highly inadequate for the job, but it would have to do. Towing it with one hand, he swam back toward the girls, coasting over the crests, stroking hard in the troughs. Josey and Chili seized the timber gratefully and he saw that they had stripped off their clothing. They were shivering. Josey's yellow hair hung to her shoulders in wet straight lines.

Rennick stopped stroking in order to rest and immediately the timber began to sink. He kicked his legs several times and the timber rose back to the surface. Again he stopped swimming and the timber began to submerge slowly, Josey looked at him, her face white, her large eyes frightened and staring. He began to swim again, keeping one hand on the timber and pushing it slowly forward, trying to keep it perpendicular with the waves. He used slow steady strokes that he hoped would conserve his energy. Occasionally a wave broke across them, roaring in his eardrums, and he heard Josey and Chili cough and spit up water. Once they were lifted by a large swell and he looked around quickly,

151

searching in the darkness for the shadow of the island. He saw it just before the swell eased them down again. The island lay far away, a low oblong of dirty blackness unrelieved by lights. He wondered if anyone on the island had seen the flames. He wondered if rescue boats would be sent and what chance they would have of being found in the darkness. He looked at the wet luminous dial of his wrist watch. Ten minutes after ten. Dawn was a long, long way off.

He swam on steadily, nausea in his belly, his brain gripped by thoughts that he tried unsuccessfully to ignore. When he supposed at least half an hour had passed, he looked again at his watch. The hands still indicated ten after ten. He wondered if the watch was broken or if he was slowly going crazy. Pictures, dark and shadowy as film negatives, loomed before his eyes and would not be washed away by the spray and the waves. Again he saw the cop and saw him falling with the bullet just below the ear. Again he saw his arm striking the busboy. He blinked his eyes, trying to shut out the things that he saw but he could not. Even more distinct than all the rest was the picture of Josey and the rifle. Josey shooting Emil. Josey shooting Michael.

Without breaking the rhythm of his strokes, he turned and looked at her. Her slim arms were hooked over the timber, her head resting on them. He reached out and put his hand on her shoulder. The flesh was cold and wet. He shook her. She raised her head slowly. He shook her again and she turned and looked at him.

"Why did you kill Michael?" he asked.

She continued to look at him, but did not answer.

He asked the question again, shouting over the sound of the waves. She shook her head and he saw her lips form two words. "I didn't . . ."

His fingers dug into the flesh of her shoulder and he shouted at her again. "Damn you, you did!"

She unhooked her arms from the timber and came to him through the water. "I didn't mean to!" She put an arm around his neck. "It was an accident—I aimed at Emil!"

"It was no accident!" Rennick shoved her arm away as

152

the piece of timber shifted awkwardly in the water. "Get over where you were or you'll drown us all!"

Ignoring the pleading in her eyes, he sent her back to her end of the timber near Chili.

He swam on and on. Despite the movement of his legs, he was cold. The chill of the water seeped far into his marrow, drove deep into muscle. He began to feel the danger signs of fatigue—a slight numbness in his fingers and a tendency to swallow water. For a few minutes he rested while the girls kicked their legs and kept the timber from submerging. But they wasted their energy with awkward thrashing and he knew they would need all their strength if they were to last out the night. He knew that the inevitable time would come when they would be too weak to even cling to the timber. And he wondered what he would do then. Once he raised his head and looked toward the island—still there were no lights. It seemed fantastic that people ashore could have failed to see the flames.

He began to swim again. Kick. Pause. Kick. Pause. He saw that Josey was watching him but he avoided her eyes. It had been foolish to expect an explanation from her about Michael. She had lied all along and she had killed Michael because he was in a position to reveal some of her lies. She had lied about being at the piano. He wondered why she lied about that when she knew her testimony could save his neck. She'd lied about the slot machine. When they'd gotten near Ventura—which was where she'd wanted to go all along—she'd made it seem natural and spontaneous when she'd suggested that they stop. She'd made the phone call that morning while he'd been asleep. She'd set the whole thing up, called Michael and Alfred and Chili, given them their instructions. He wondered how she felt now, knowing that all her precious plans were at the bottom of the Pacific.

He glanced at her again. Her head was bowed on her arms and it nodded wearily on her shoulders as the timber rose and fell with the water. Faintly he could see the delicate curve of her ear and the clean line of her white shoulder. With the curl gone from her hair and her make-up washed away, she looked like a child, a young girl, and he knew that despite everything that had happened he still loved her. He couldn't understand it.

153

He swam on and on, one hand pushing the timber. Long ago his fingers had forgotten the pain of the splinters. He wondered how long it had been since the yacht sank. Two hours? Two days? He tried to recall details of the chart that had been aboard the Chris-Craft. The boats had gone down about twelve miles from the island. There had been a current indicated on the chart. But had the current swept in toward the island or away from it? Was the current taking them toward the island or away from it?

He felt the tiny pinch of danger in his left calf that meant a cramp was forming. Again he rested, clinging to the timber and ducking his head under his arm so he could breathe without sucking in spray. The girls were too tired to thrash their legs more than a minute. He began to swim again and the warning in his calf became more urgent. Favoring the leg, he let it trail limply in the water while he stroked with his right leg and his right arm. He was just barely able to keep the timber at the surface of the water. His right leg began to tire and he decided to test his left leg again.

After less than three kicks, the full grip of the cramp caught him. It was like a sharp blade deep in the muscle. He groaned with the pain. He let go of the timber, seized his calf and sank briefly under water as he massaged the muscle and pounded it with his fist in an effort to relieve the stiffness.

When he surfaced, he saw that Josey had left the timber and was swimming weakly toward him. She cried out his name once.

"John!"

"I'm okay!" he said angrily.

Taking her arm, he towed her back to the timber. Then he floated nearby on his back, massaging his leg until the soreness was nearly gone. When he turned over and swam to the timber he noticed that it bore the weight of the two girls although neither was swimming to help buoy it up. He realized that it was his own weight that caused the timber to sink. As he watched, Chili's head dipped wearily forward and her hands loosened their grip on the wood. He slapped her bare shoulder sharply. She shook her head and regained her grip but it was obvious how tired she was. A plan began to form in Rennick's brain, a plan he tried to resist. But

154

its logic was too strong to resist. The island was still many miles away and he knew he was no long-distance swimmer. The timber could support two people—but not three. Why shouldn't those two be him and Josey?

Again he glanced at Chili. Her head was bowing and once more her fingers were beginning to slide along the wet sides of the timber. It would be easy to ignore her. Half unconscious, she wouldn't even know it when she slipped under. He watched her from the corner of his eye, watched a wave buffet her away from the timber. Her back struck the cross-arm and her arms hung limply in the water.

Why not? Why shouldn't he and Josey have the chance? Why shouldn't Josey testify for him, clear him of the charge of killing the cop?

But even as he asked himself the questions his hand was reaching out, slapping Chili on the shoulder, awakening her and pushing her back to safety. She looked at him, a look of pure gratitude, and he turned away ashamed, unable to meet her eyes.

Moving his legs automatically, he swam on. He had never been so tired in his life. Coils of fatigue were twisting around his leg muscles and his shoulder muscles, squeezing the life out of them. He wanted to sleep. He wanted to stretch out somewhere, rest his legs and sleep. It would be so easy to sleep in the water. Just let go of the timber, relax his legs and go to sleep. They said drowning was easy once you were unconscious. The timber would keep the girls afloat, and what right did he have to live anyway? A life for a life, a tooth for a tooth. He had killed and now he would die and the ledger would at last be balanced.

Abruptly something struck him in the side, something soft and cold, and he realized it was Josey and she had lost her grip on the timber. She clung to him weakly, her bare legs tangling in his. He shouted at her, cuffed her cheeks until her eyes opened, and shoved her back so she could grasp the timber again. Then he began to swim again, kicking his legs slowly, resting a moment now and then when he felt the familiar pinch of the cramp in his left calf.

It was obvious that he would have to hang on. Without him, the girls would be lost. They were too weak to take care of themselves.

155

Time passed. Once he raised his head and looked at the island. It was no closer than it had been before. And still there were no lights.

The cramp was getting worse and his pauses to massage it were becoming more frequent. Each time he found it harder to float on his back in order to massage his leg. The muscle of his right leg was beginning to sound a warning also and it would be only a matter of time until it grew worse.

Two. The word impressed itself over and over on his brain to the point where it was impossible to ignore it.

Two.

Two could float with the timber but three could not.

Why shouldn't he save Chili? Why shouldn't he do one decent thing in his life? She had killed no one, she had hurt no one. Of the three of them, she alone deserved to live.

But that meant Josey would have to go.

Suddenly he remembered the little man who had sat on the bench in the park, the little man with "God First" written on his hat. "Are you ready, sinner?" the old man had asked. "Are you ready to die?" And the old man had been right. Emil had been a sinner and Emil had died. Vodka had been a sinner and she had died. Sutro and Stanley and Michael had been sinners and they had died. Josey was a sinner . . .

But he knew he couldn't do it. He couldn't let Josey die.

Kicking his legs weakly, he swam on. The timber was just barely afloat. For the hundredth time he shifted his grip and began to stroke with his left arm. The water sucked at his fingers, refusing to let them pass through. When he tried to stroke harder, he felt the beginning of a cramp in his shoulder. Cramps in his legs and now in his shoulder—it wouldn't be long now. He rested his chin for a moment on the timber and through a wave that washed over them saw a pale hand reach out. It reached out toward Chili. It was Josey's hand and he watched, fascinated, as it groped for Chili's shoulder. Chili's grip on the timber had loosened again and only a touch would be needed to send her away. He saw Josey's hand strike Chili, pushing her off.

"No!" he roared.

Seizing Chili by the hair, he shook her roughly and dragged her back. He slapped her face until he was sure she was awake and able to hold on again. He heard Josey weeping almost hysterically and when she looked at him he stared back steadily and he knew that she understood him. She cried for a long time, her shoulders trembling, her head resting on her arms. After a while she stopped crying and her head began to rock weakly on her shoulders from the motion of the waves. She slipped down a little farther in the water but caught herself and pulled herself back up. In another moment, her head fell forward again and her fingers slipped stiffly across the wet surface of the timber. One hand fell away and she turned limply as a wave washed across her.

He looked up into the black sky and he felt something tearing within him. "God" he said, "give me strength. Give me strength to let her go!"

When he looked again at her place on the timber, she was gone.

He looked at the waves around them but he could not see her. He screamed like an animal and swam away from the timber but he could not find her. He dived under the timber and behind it, pawing at the water, but he could not find her.

When his muscles were so stiff and full of pain that he could no longer dive, he worked his way feebly back to the timber. He hooked one arm around it and clung there, retching salt water and spit, trying to forget what he had done but knowing already that he would never forget, whether he lived for another minute or a hundred years.

He did not know how long he hung onto the timber. Time lost all meaning for him. There was a long dark period in which he was aware of the tremendous cold of the ocean, a cold that froze the very blood in his veins and turned his arm, where it was locked around the timber, into a numb stiffness that was beyond all movement. For a while he was aware that his other arm was hooked some way around Chili, but he was not sure about this, nor did he have enough strength left to open his eyes and see whether she was fact or fancy. He wanted to sleep.

He woke very slowly, disturbed by the strange warmth that played across his naked shoulders. He moved nothing but his eyes. He saw a blurry gray carpet. He studied it a long, long while before he realized that the carpet was a

157

sandy beach and he was lying on it. When he tried to move, his body was a huge pain. He turned his head and saw that his arm was still locked around the timber. The timber was dry and so were the strands of dark green seaweed that coiled around the wooden crossarm and around the throat of Chili who lay nearby face down.

Seeing Chili, he remembered.

With an effort that left him weak and sick to his stomach, he sat up and looked around him, shielding his eyes from the bright sun. They were on the island. He looked out at the ocean. The water was a clean, clear blue and the smooth-running waves gave no hint of the agony of the long night.

She was still out there. And he had left her there.

He lowered his head and covered his face with his dry swollen hands. It was not that she could have told the court the truth of what had happened when the cop was killed. It was not the tenderness of her mouth and the sweetness of her body. It was simply that he had loved her.

He turned and fell against the sand. For many minutes he lay there. He did not move again until he felt the movement of Chili as she struggled to sit up. When he looked at her she was trying to draw the tight strands of seaweed away from her throat and down from where they were tangled in her damp dark hair. She was too weak to conceal her nakedness from him. Impersonally he looked at her slim tanned body, the curve of her hips and the triangle of blondness. He glanced up at the short brunette curls where the seaweed was tangled and then down at her blondness and he began to laugh.

He laughed for a long time, bitter crazy laughter that hurt his throat. Then he became silent.

When he spoke, he did not look at her. "You're a blonde," he said. "A natural blonde."

"Yes," she said.

"You were the girl at the piano in the lounge. You saw me kill the cop."

"Yes."

He began to laugh again. "You crazy fool! Why didn't you tell me?"

"I didn't trust . . . you." She coughed, weakly spitting up water from her lungs. "They made me dye my hair."

"And you know Georgetti?"

She waited a moment before replying. "Josey was Georgetti . . ."

He turned and looked at her then and this time he did not laugh. "Josey?"

She nodded. "Georgetti was the name we used for whoever was in charge. For a long time Emil was Georgetti and then later when Josey turned against him she became Georgetti . . ."

They were silent. He looked out at the smooth blue ocean and then he looked away.

Her fingers touched his arm. "You saved my life, John, and—"

"Don't call me John," he said harshly.

She hesitated. "You saved my life and I can never repay you . . . but I can testify for you. And I can tell them that Emil killed Rudolpho because I was there in the kitchen when he did it. Later Emil locked me in the closet because he was afraid I might talk."

Rennick stared at her. "Emil killed the busboy?"

"Rudolpho was in love with Laurette. I was there when Stanley told Emil that Rudolpho had been in Laurette's room a few times. Emil went looking for the boy, found him in the kitchen after you had knocked him out and . . . he finished the job."

Rennick began to laugh again.

"Must you," she said. "Must you laugh like that?"

"My god!" he said. "Don't you see how funny it is? Don't you see how you've ruined it?"

He rolled over and struck the sand with his swollen fist. "When I let her go, I thought I was letting myself go. I thought for once in my life I was doing something decent. I thought I was hanging myself . . ."

He looked at Chili. "Don't you see how you've ruined it? She's gone and I'm alive. And I'm not going to die!"

Turning, he gazed out at the smooth blue ocean.

www.ingramcontent.com/pod-product-compliance
Lightning Source LLC
Chambersburg PA
CBHW020134180626
46810CB00004B/1546